# INFINITE MAGIC

Dragon's Gift: The Huntress Book 5

Linsey Hall

# DEDICATION

For Rob and Lauren, an amazing couple.

# ACKNOWLEDGMENTS

The Dragon's Gift series is a product of my two lives: one as an archaeologist and one as a novelist. Combining these two took a bit of work. I'd like to thank my friends, Wayne Lusardi, the State Maritime Archaeologist for Michigan, and Douglas Inglis and Veronica Morris, both archaeologists for Interactive Heritage, for their ideas about how to have a treasure hunter heroine that doesn't conflict too much with archaeology's ethics. The Author's Note contains a bit more about this if you are interested.

Thank you, Ben, for everything you've done to support me in this career. Thank you to Emily Keane for giving me the inspiration for Emile, Ralph, and Rufus. Thank you to Carol Thomas for sharing your thoughts on the book and being amazing inspiration.

Thank you to Jena O'Connor and Lindsey Loucks for various forms of editing. The book is immensely better because of you! And thank you to Rebecca Frank for the beautiful cover. You really bring Cass to life.

# CHAPTER ONE

Prison sucked. No two ways about it, two hots and a cot was as bad as I'd feared. Not that I actually got two hots at the Prison for Magical Miscreants. Food at this lovely establishment left a lot to be desired. And my cot had one skinny blanket, which did nothing to ward off the chill that came through the tiny, open window set high in the wall.

I shivered against the cold and rubbed the goosebumps off my arms. The regulation black shirt and pants the prison staff had given me were basically worthless for warmth.

It was a good thing I'd be busting out of here soon, or I'd lose my mind. I hadn't seen another person in the three days I'd been here, unless I counted the hand that shoved a bowl of gruel through the hole in the door twice a day. I should count myself lucky for that, actually. They could be coming to torture me for information instead of coming to feed me.

But what I wouldn't give for a Pabst Blue Ribbon and a Cornish Pasty from my friends' shop back home. Just the thought of my friends made my heart clench in my chest.

A faint rustling sounded from behind me and I turned. A fat black and white rat ran through the hole in the stone wall. I grinned at the sight of Rufus, who was an emissary for my buddy Emile, an Anima Mage who was locked up in another cell. Our cells were just stone boxes with wooden doors, none of that wall of bars business so popular on TV, so I'd never seen Emile in person.

I could see him through Rufus, though. I shifted from where I sat on the bed and lowered my hand so that the little rat could jump onto it.

Rufus hopped on, and his warm weight and tiny little paws were the best thing I'd felt the whole time I'd been here. Another being—someone who wasn't out to get me and didn't care that I was a FireSoul—was a welcome distraction from this hell hole.

"Hey, buddy," I said.

Rufus stood up on his hind legs and twitched his pink nose, his gaze on mine. I grinned as a vision of Emile filled my head, sent by Rufus through his brother Ralph. Ralph was in Emile's cell, looking at Emile. My new friend's Anima Mage powers created a connection between the four of us.

As usual, Emile was sitting on his bed, his skinny form curled against the cold. He had dark hair and eyes, and though I could make out his face, the vision wasn't very clear.

Emile was getting weaker and sicker, and I suspected it was because he fed most of his rations to Ralph and Rufus. I'd started sharing with them, too, though the little rats could really scarf down some gruel.

We needed to escape soon because I didn't think Emile would make it much longer. And I was sure they weren't going to just leave me in here. Something worse was waiting for me.

"Hey, Emile," I said. "Got some good news for me?"

"Yeah," Emile said. "And some bad news."

I grimaced. Bad news in a place like this was usually *bad.* "Start with the bad."

"My trial date has been set for day after tomorrow."

"Shit." Emile was a FireSoul like me. We were the most despised type of immortal, hunted and destroyed because we possessed the ability to steal another's powers when we killed them. No one cared that most FireSouls had never stolen a power in their life.

I'd taken powers, but only when a person offered or from people who were trying to kill me. Though guilt still crawled up my back with little claws when I thought of it. I tried to shake it away.

"Morning or night?" I asked, calculating the time we had left to escape. I wouldn't leave here without Emile.

"Not sure."

"Okay, then we assume morning. Have you heard anything about a potential trial date for me?" Like me, Emile wasn't allowed to leave his cell. He heard things through Ralph and Rufus when they went on scouting missions.

"No. I still don't think they know you're a FireSoul. And I also don't think they know your name. They normally refer to us by our last names, but they call you Prisoner 857."

"Weird." I'd been captured a week ago while trying to rescue my best friends from a sociopath called Victor Orriodor. A member of the Order of the Magica—the government that ruled all magic users—had witnessed the rescue attempt. I'd gotten my friends out, but had been captured by the Order member's guards after I'd used some serious magic against them. "I have no idea why he wouldn't tell the prison what I am."

"Just be grateful," Emile said. "You don't have a trial date yet."

"Yeah. I don't know why no one has come to interrogate me, but I'll take it."

"Breaking your spirit," he said. "They'll come soon enough."

I grimaced. Emile was likely looking at execution. "I'll get us out of here before that happens."

"Do you have backup coming?" he asked.

I hoped not. Del and Nix, my best friends who were really my sisters by choice, were also FireSouls. I called them my *deirfiúr*, sisters in our native Irish. Though I knew they would stage a rescue attempt, I didn't want them to risk getting tossed in here, too. I could get myself out just fine.

I hoped.

"We need to assume that no help is coming. But I've got a plan. Did Ralph and Rufus see where the guards are keeping my stuff?"

"Yeah, that's the good news." Emile gave me directions to the room where they stored prisoners' belongings before auctioning them off, doing his best to paint a picture of the prison that was outside my cell walls. I'd been brought here while mostly unconscious, so I had little memory of the layout. "Do you really need that stuff? It's all the way across the prison. We should just run for it. And how are we getting out anyway?"

"Yeah, I need that stuff. I'm not letting them take anything else from me." They had my daggers, a gift from my boyfriend, Aidan. But it was more than sentimentality. "And they took a transport charm and a Penatrist charm from me."

"Whoa," Emile said.

"Exactly. I want those back." Penatrist charms were super valuable and insanely rare. They helped you break through protection spells, both getting in and getting out. Like the protection spells on a prison. The transport charm would blast us right out of here. We needed both if we wanted to escape.

"Be ready, Emile," I said. "I'll get you out of here."

He nodded, then the connection blanked out.

"Thanks, buddy," I said to Rufus as I set him on the ground near my gruel bowl. I'd saved some for him, and he started chowing down. "We'll feed you better when we get out of here."

Rufus didn't respond, but he did look up, gruel on his whiskers. I grinned, then leaned against the cold wall of my prison cell and turned my attention inward, focusing on my magic.

I shouldn't be able to access my power here—the prison was enchanted to block magic—but as of last week, I was the most powerful Magica in the world.

True, I didn't have much control over my magic, but that would come. Right now, I was basically a fire hydrant of power that was trying to blow out of a straw. The result was usually an explosion.

But in here, the prison's spells dampened enough of my power that I could actually control it. They'd crush a normal Magica's powers. A prison that allowed its magical inhabitants to use their gifts wouldn't be very effective.

Emile shouldn't be able to use his, but there were exceptions to every rule. My theory was that Emile's power drew from the animal's innate magic, so he had a source of power outside of himself.

Whatever made it possible, I was grateful. Ralph and Rufus were little scouts and emissaries that were vastly improving our chances at escape.

Magic thrummed in my veins, humming along my skin. I had a number of gifts to choose from, all of them stolen at some point in the last couple months.

As a result, I was loaded for bear. I was a Mirror Mage, able to mimic another supernatural's gifts, and a wolf shifter. I could send lightning shooting out of my fingertips and create illusions. Now I just had to figure out how to use these to get out of my cell.

Lightning could fry the wooden door, but I didn't want to alert the guards with the thunder that followed. And would my lightning even be strong enough? The way my magic was dampened, I thought maybe not.

That meant I was going to have to mirror the power of whatever supernatural came to deliver dinner. I'd been biding my time, waiting for a useful magical gift, but one hadn't showed up yet. Now it seemed I was running out of time.

I went over Emile's description of the prison in my head, testing out scenarios. I hoped the dinner guard was telekinetic. That'd be ace. I could just manipulate the lock in the door to click it open.

When footsteps sounded in the hall, I jerked upright, my eyes flaring open. It was too early for dinner. And no one walked down this hall outside of meal times. The figures were still fairly far away—all the way down the hall if I had to guess.

I strained my hearing, trying to count the number of people coming down the hall. My hearing had been astoundingly good since I'd unlocked my root power. Even better than the improved hearing I'd gotten when I'd taken a wolf Shifter's power.

Three pairs of footsteps. No, four. One was heavier than the rest, his footsteps plodding.

My heart thundered as I waited. When they stopped in front of my door, deadly calm descended over me. This was it. Whatever the reason four people were at my cell, I wasn't going to like it.

A key scraped against the keyhole. Part of me wanted to hide behind the door and jump them, but my advantage was in stealth. They didn't know I could use my powers. Though I wasn't at full strength, it was an incredible advantage.

I reached out for their magical signatures, hoping to get an early hint at their gifts. What would I be working with?

A sickly sweet smell hit my nose and I stiffened. *The bulldog.* The Order member who'd sent me to this prison had magic that smelled like that. I'd called him the bulldog for his size and heavy jowls. He was a powerful weather witch who could also create magical shields.

When the door creaked open, I held my breath. The bulldog stepped in, his piercing blue eyes going straight for me. I stiffened and glared at him. He was about sixty, dressed in a snappy suit and sporting a lumbering gait that would put someone at ease before they realized how powerful he was.

Three men accompanied him. Two Magica entered behind him. They had hulking shoulders and mean-looking faces. I reached out for their magical signature, trying to get a feel for their gifts. One felt ephemeral. Invisibility. Cool. The other felt like shocks in my bloodstream. This guy could shoot stunning spells.

I'd have to be careful of him. They all wore a heavy metal bracelet. From the feel of their magic, which wasn't repressed by the cell, the bracelets made them immune to the prison's dampening spells, allowing them to use their magic.

That wasn't good for me.

A slender man trailed behind them, pale and gaunt. His gaze was even colder than the bulldog's, and he too wore a heavy silver bracelet. I shivered.

But then his power signature hit me. It felt like tiny bubbles in my head. Not a good feeling, not a bad one.

He was a Mind Mage.

I tried to school my features into placidity as I stared at the men. I needed time to get a handle on everyone's powers so I could use them to my advantage. Particularly the Mind Mage's. They all had different gifts over people's minds, and I didn't know what his was.

I also wanted to know what the bulldog was up to. He'd been colluding with Victor Orriodor, the sociopath from whom I'd rescued my *deirfiúr*. Victor wanted me and my *deirfiúr* for some unknown, terrible purpose. I wanted to know what it was.

"Where are your friends?" the bulldog demanded.

I laughed at him, but my heart lightened at the knowledge that he still didn't know their names. He was Order of the Magica. If he knew their names, he'd be able to find them in an instant.

He stared at me stonily.

So I laughed some more, then finally choked it back and asked, "Wait, you're serious? You expect me to actually tell you where they are?"

He flicked his fingers, and the Mind Mage stepped forward. "You know what he is?"

"An ugly cretin who's thrown his lot in with a slime trail like you?" But I eyed the Mind Mage warily.

"He's a Mind Mage. His specialty is the thalamus." The bulldog's disparaging gaze swept over me. "You're clever. I'm sure you can figure out what that means."

The thalamus was one of the pain centers of the brain. Damn. I didn't really want to mess with that kind of power. I was a thief, not a torturer.

"Yeah, yeah. You'll try to torture me into telling you." Which actually made my stomach heave, but I couldn't let him know that. I'd have to be careful trying to get some answers, though. If his Mind Mage got to me before I launched my offensive, I'd be screwed. But I could probably poke a bit more. "Wouldn't it just be a better idea to convince me to be on your side? Because I can guarantee you can't force the info out of me."

"No?" His gaze was icy.

"Obviously not. I'd gladly die before giving up my friends. And you can't guarantee you'll get the truth out of me anyway." I flicked imaginary dust off the shoulder of my prison jumpsuit and glanced back up at him. "I'm sure Victor has told you about me. I'm not your ordinary Magica. He couldn't get what he wanted from me when I was just a kid. You definitely won't be able to now."

"We have our ways."

"Yeah, yeah. That guy." My gaze rested on the Mind Mage as I continued to gather up his power and that of the Invisibility Mage. It was swelling inside my chest, ready to be let free. "Why don't you just tell me what Victor wants us for. And why you're allied with him? Do the rest of the Order of the Magica know what I am?"

His gaze cut coldly to mine. "They will if I don't get what I want."

So he was going to stick with the threats. But even those gave me valuable info. Whatever the bulldog was up to, the rest of the Order of the Magica didn't know about it. He was operating behind their back.

I'd suspected it, but the confirmation was literally the best piece of news I'd had all month.

The two guards stepped back toward the door, blocking it. The bulldog's right hand flicked toward the Mind Mage, then gestured toward me.

*Out of time.*

I reached out for the guards' invisibility and stunning powers. They were both elusive strains of magic. One felt like mist and the other sent little electric shocks over my skin, but I got a grip on their gifts.

"How about some incent—"

I cut off his words by throwing a blast of stunning magic at him. The magic shot from my fingers as a glittery blue streak. The bulldog crashed to his knees, his eyes rolling back in his head before he fell to his side.

The Mind Mage's pale gaze met mine, surprise in their depths. *Didn't expect me to have my magic, did ya?*

I called upon the invisibility gift just as he raised his hand to hit me with his magic. My skin felt shivery and wet as the magic raced over my arms and legs, concealing me from everyone in the room.

I couldn't see my hands! It'd worked.

The Mind Mage's brows jumped as I disappeared fully. With a glance at the guards, I lunged off the bed, trying to stay silent. My bare feet helped.

The burly guards rushed forward, their heads whipping around, searching for me. The Mind Mage looked as well, his gaze wide as he raised his hands to send his awful magic at me.

I shot a stunning spell at him, the blue magic streaking from my fingers. I lunged to the side, trying to conceal my position now that the blue magic had given me away. The Mind Mage crashed to the ground, then lay still as a rock.

I struggled to hold on to the invisibility as I edged around the room. With the prison's magic dampening ability, I didn't have full access to my power. I was running low and would be visible soon.

With one last surge of effort, I reached for the last of my power and sent a stunning spell at each of the guards.

When the big men crashed to the ground, I leapt up and ran for the door. I hesitated over the bulldog's prone form, staring down at his jowly face. He had evil intentions for me and my *deirfiúr*. I could kill him now. Whatever he had planned for us was probably worth killing him over. The support he provided Victor was bad enough.

But he was incapacitated. And I believed in fair fights. So did my *deirfiúr*. And I had to prove I didn't belong in prison. Killing folks wouldn't help that. The Order of the Magica would already be after me, even though they didn't know my name. I didn't need to add killing to the list of reasons they thought I should be locked up.

I'd never done anything really wrong before. My tomb raiding followed all the laws for the proper disposal of dangerous magical artifacts, so I wasn't really a thief. And I only killed demons, which was allowed, or those actively out to kill me.

I couldn't ruin my good name. And killing a defenseless guy might actually ruin my soul.

But I could definitely use that silver bracelet around his wrist. If I had full access to my power, I'd have no trouble getting out of here.

I crouched down and tugged on the bracelet, careful not to touch the bulldog's sallow skin.

It didn't budge. I frowned as I spun the thing on his wrist, searching for the clasp. It was a heavy silver piece, almost like a cuff. At the back was a tiny hole for a key.

Damn it. They'd locked the things on. Probably to keep things like this from happening. I gave it a few more tugs, trying to pull the bracelet off his wrist, but it didn't budge. His fist was just too big.

Well, shit. That wasn't going to work. Looked like I'd be doing this the hard way. But I could feel their magical signatures despite the fact they were passed out. They could come in handy later, so I gathered up a bit of each person's magical gift, feeling out their signatures and drawing a piece of it into me.

As a Mirror Mage, I could use their magic while I was near them. Or I could store up a little bit to be used later. I'd only have enough for one spell, but that was better than nothing.

I stood and left him where he lay, then crept into the hall, my feet silent on the stone floor. Just because I'd defeated the bulldog and his goons didn't mean there weren't other guards lurking.

Quietly, I shut the door behind me, locking them into my cell. If I was lucky, it'd be a while before they woke or any of the other guards found them.

Heart in my throat, I glanced around. The stone hallway was dimly lit with flickering yellow bulbs that hung from bare wires. The prison was old, and the renovation to add electricity had obviously been done with a budget in mind. Heavy wooden doors dotted the hall, each with a small hatch at the bottom for food delivery.

Emile's cell was at one end, and my belongings were in a room on the other side of the building. We'd agreed that I'd get my stuff first and come back for him. He was no good in a fight, he'd said. I wouldn't make him risk himself, and if he really was as bad as he'd said, he'd be a liability.

I set off down the hall, sticking close to the wall in case someone appeared. It wouldn't give me much advantage, but it was all I had.

Every now and again, I'd hear rustling from inside a cell. I couldn't see into them, but the feeling of the occupant's repressed magical signature made me shudder. Whoever was locked up here deserved it. This place housed FireSouls and real criminals. Murderers and monsters. I wouldn't feel bad about *not* helping them escape.

Footsteps sounded from ahead. I froze, my gaze riveted to where a new hallway joined the one in which I stood. I tried the door handle nearest me, but it didn't budge.

The hair on my arms stood on end. *Shit, shit, shit.* There was nowhere to hide.

I reached inside myself for the invisibility gift that I'd taken from one of the guards, shivering as the magic raced over my skin. The damp feeling was still there, which was awful combined with the prison's chill air.

When I glanced down at myself, all I saw was the stone wall and floor. It'd worked.

And not a moment too soon.

Three guards turned the corner, headed in my direction. They were all big men with squashed-looking faces. Some kind of troll maybe. They each wore a heavy silver bracelet.

So they were big *and* they had use of whatever magical gift they owned.

I held my breath and pressed myself against the wall as they passed, praying they couldn't hear the beat of my heart. It thundered so loudly in my ears, I was certain they had to hear it.

The smallest one—who was still a good foot taller than me—hesitated as he passed me, his blunt nose twitching as if he smelled something.

Shit. I hadn't had a bath in days. If he didn't smell my magic, he definitely smelled my BO. I was ripe as an avocado left out in the sun.

"Brar? You coming?" one of the other guards asked.

He shook his head as if to clear it, then started walking again, following his friends. "You need to take a shower, Merk," he said. "You smell like the underside of a hog's belly."

Merk laughed, the booming sound echoing off the stone walls.

My heart had climbed all the way up into my throat, making it impossible to breathe. I was so freaked out by his hesitation near me that it took me a moment to realize he'd mistaken my BO for his friend's. My shoulders nearly sagged in relief as they turned a corner up ahead.

I almost grinned, thanking my awful odor and the lack of bathing facilities in the cell, then continued on, deciding to hold on to the invisibility as long as I could. If I dropped it now, I'd never pick it up again.

I nearly jumped when something tiny scurried in front of me.

*Ralph.*

He turned and twitched his little pink nose at me, as if he were finding me by scent, then he turned and ran off down the hall.

*Thank you, Emile.*

My friend must have realized I was trying to escape and sent Ralph to lead me to the room where they stored my stuff.

With Ralph leading the way, I reached the room a few minutes later. Fortunately, I hadn't run into any more guards.

But there was one sitting at a little desk in the tiny room stuffed full of prisoners' belongings. The woman had a mean look to her face, with drawn brows and pinched lips.

She looked up when I stepped into the room. Her eyes widened.

"Hey!" She raised a hand as if to shoot me with magic.

My invisibility charm must have run out. I called on the last of the stunning power I'd borrowed from the guard, letting it tingle all the way to my fingertips, and zapped her. She hit the ground before the glittery blue streak of magic faded away.

"Looks like I'm leaving a trail of bodies behind me," I whispered to Ralph, who ran to one of the shelves and climbed up the side.

I followed him with my gaze, grinning when I spotted my twin obsidian daggers. They'd always been my favorite weapon, though these were replacements from Aidan for the original pair I'd lost.

I grabbed them off the shelf, noting a paper tag that said *Prisoner 857*. My gaze skated across the shelf full of objects. Other items were tagged with names.

So they really didn't have my name. Which gave me a temporary reprieve. *Thank magic.*

Quickly, I searched for my charms. I'd had my comms charm on me when I'd been taken, along with a transport charm and a Penatrist charm. My escape relied on the last two, though I wanted the first one back as well.

I found my comms charm shoved on the back of the shelf, along with the Penatrist charm. I grabbled the golden necklace and the small black rock. Next to them was the wide golden cuff that possessed a dampening charm. I'd worn it to control my massive new power. Until I learned to wield my new magic, I'd need that. I took it, too.

But no matter where I looked, I couldn't find the transport charm.

There were no other transport charms, either. Victor Orriodor had been hunting and collecting them. Perhaps the shortage had reached even here. Or they stored them elsewhere.

My stomach dropped as I continued to search, growing more and more frantic as I shoved things around on the shelves. The transport charm was my only surefire way out—otherwise we'd have to leave on foot. I wasn't sure where the Prison for Magical Miscreants was located, but from the cold air that always seeped through the little window in my cell, it was somewhere chilly. And probably remote.

*Shit, shit, shit.* Changing tactics, I searched for clothes or boots. If I had to run for it, Emile and I would at least need shoes. But it appeared they'd discarded all our clothes and footwear. Those weren't worth auctioning off, apparently. Apparently they didn't know what my boots were actually worth.

A shuffling noise sounded from behind me, cutting through my distraction. I stiffened and turned.

Eight guards stood in the doorway.

Trapped.

With no way to escape.

# CHAPTER TWO

A guard threw a stunning spell. The glittery blue magic streaked toward me, and I dodged just in time, throwing myself behind the desk. The woman who'd originally guarded the room was still passed out on the floor. She hadn't alerted the guards, which meant they'd found the bodies in my cell.

I clutched my daggers, debating my options.

But there was only one option.

Fight.

Even then, I was screwed. Me against eight guards using my limited magic? And the guards were Magica and Shifters, not demons. I didn't want to kill them.

But I also couldn't go back to that cell. Not just for my own sake, but for Emile's. And for my *deirfiúr*.

This was going to be tough.

"Better get out of here," I whispered to Rufus. "Don't want you to get hit in the crossfire."

The little rat twitched his nose, but didn't run.

"Suit yourself." I peered around the side of the desk and flung Righty at the guard nearest me. The obsidian flashed in the light as it flew. It thudded into the guard's thigh, and he stumbled to the ground.

He howled and clutched his leg.

Quickly, I nicked the back of my wrist with Lefty, using my blood to ignite the spell that would call Righty back to me.

Righty pulled itself from the guard's leg, but before it could fly back to me, another guard snatched it out of the air. He'd moved so fast!

Righty struggled to pull itself free of his grip, but it didn't work.

A stunning spell crashed into the wall behind me, missing me by a millimeter.

Damn it. My daggers clearly weren't going to do the job.

I called upon my power, reaching out for the guard's gift over stunning spells. I got ahold of his magic, which smelled oddly of cleaning products, and peeked out from behind the desk.

When I had a guard in my sight, I threw the stunning spell at him. The glittery blue magic streaked through the air and hit him in the chest. He collapsed like an oak, falling flat onto his face.

"The prisoner has her power!" a guard called. "Shields!"

*Shit.*

I peeked out, ready to throw another stunning spell, and caught sight of the guards reaching toward their backs and pulling shields out. They must have been holstered back there. I managed to get a stunning spell off and hit one guard in the side before the line of shields appeared in front of them.

They were now an impenetrable line. Maybe I could hit them on their exposed knees, but I wasn't sure how much good that would do. If I had access to all of my magic, I could create a massive stunning spell to blast through their shields. But I didn't. There might be a lake of power within me, but I could only sip it out with a straw.

Blasts of magic pounded the desk as they approached, throwing stunning spells. I reached out with my magic, feeling for their signatures. Maybe there was something more useful than stunning spells.

I got a whiff of smoke from a Fire Mage. Nope, no good. This stone prison wouldn't burn. And even if it did, I couldn't burn all the prisoners alive. There was an Ice Mage as well. *Working with all the elements, here, eh boys?*

There were four Shifters, but they were all big animals and none had wings. I didn't want to shift and make myself a bigger target.

"Prisoner 857, you are surrounded. Come out now."

Ha. Yeah, okay. I'd put my hands up and come out peacefully.

As if.

I searched the rest of their signatures, trying to find something more useful than stunning, the elements, or shifting.

And found none.

Shit. There was a really good chance I was going to have to go back to my cell. And the bulldog wasn't going to be nice this time around. Considering that he'd been about to torture me, I didn't want to know what his *not nice* was.

*Shit, shit, shit.*

Ralph squeaked, and I glanced at him. His black eyes were trained on something over my head. I looked up, and my jaw slackened.

A sparkling red dragonet fluttered over my head for just a second before charging the guards. A blue dragonet appeared a half second later. Like the fire dragonet, the water dragonet was the size of a cat. He charged the guards, too.

My heart leapt.

Backup had arrived.

Shouts sounded from the guards. In quick succession, the brown stone dragonet and the gray air dragonet had appeared and charged my enemy.

I hopped to my feet, my obsidian daggers ready to fly.

When I saw my friends gathered behind the guards, throwing potion bombs, my heart felt like it might fly out of my chest. They all wore masks, but it was clear that Del, Nix, Aidan, Connor, and Claire had come to save me.

Brilliant, jewel-toned liquid exploded on the guards' chests from the potion bombs. The dragonets dive-bombed their heads, knocking them down. It took them only moments to cut down all the guards, who appeared to be passed out.

I was glad they'd chosen non-lethal weapons. Though the guards had planned to put me back in my cell, they hadn't been out for my death.

"Come on!" Del called. "Let's get out of here."

I picked up Ralph and clutched him to my stomach, shielding him, then ran to my friends, jumping over the fallen bodies. I swooped down and grabbed Righty from the hand of the guard who'd caught it, then joined my friends.

I could identify which masked friend was which by their height and eyes, which peered through black ski masks.

"We've been dressing up like cat burglars too much lately," I said.

"For real," Nix said. "But we need to get out of here."

"I've got to get my friends Emile and Rufus."

"Lead the way," Aidan said.

I appreciated that they didn't question. "This way."

I led the way down the hall, sprinting full out. We no longer had stealth on our side. Speed was the only way.

When we raced by the door to my cell, it was still closed and locked. Were the bulldog and his goons still inside? I wasn't going to stop and find out.

A moment later, I skidded to a halt in front of Emile's cell door. We didn't have a key, and even though Aidan could probably knock the damned thing down, I didn't want to make more of a ruckus.

"Any chance you can transport, Del?" I asked.

"No. The prison's dampening charms are too strong."

"I'll try to mirror your gift, then," I said.

Her brows rose in surprise, but I didn't bother to explain. I called upon my power, reaching out for Del's transport gift. Her signature hit me first—the scent of fresh laundry and the feel of grass beneath my feet. When I caught hold of her ability, I grasped onto it and drew it inside myself.

I knocked on the door and yelled, "I'm coming in, Emile!"

I gave him a sec, then teleported into the cell. I almost bumped into Emile, who had his ear pressed to the door. Ralph sat on his shoulder.

"Cass!" he said.

"Come on!" I grabbed his arm and teleported back into the hall, joining my friends. "We're ready to go."

"Where's Ralph?" Aidan asked. "You said you had another friend."

I pointed to the rat who rode on Emile's shoulder. "That's Ralph." Then I held up Rufus, who I'd been clutching to my stomach. "This is Rufus."

"Of course you've become friends with rats," Del said.

"Just call me Cinderella." I glanced down either end of the hall, then looked at my friends "How'd you get in?"

"Through the kitchen delivery door, using the Penatrist charm," Aidan said. "Follow me."

We set off running, Aidan leading the way down the hall. The dragonets flew beside us. My heart pounded in my ears, a fierce staccato. Every shadow and tiny noise sounded to me like the guards were coming. The cell doors flashed by as we raced for the exit.

"Right," Aidan said when we reached a crossroads in the hall.

We turned and ran smack into Merk, Brar, and his buddy. The troll guards I'd passed earlier. Shit.

Their eyebrows popped up in surprise, but before they could raise the alarm, the dragonets charged them. The stone dragonet slammed into Merk's ugly face, knocking him over, while the air dragonet plowed into Brar, a mini cyclone of wind that threw him into the wall. His big head thunked against it and he collapsed.

The water dragonet splashed against the face of the last troll. As he was choking on water, Aidan stepped forward and punched him square in the face. His eyes rolled back in his ugly head, and he fell onto his back, crashing against the ground.

"Nice one," I said as I checked to make sure they were all passed out. They were. Good.

Aidan shook out his fist. "I've had some pent up aggression since you were taken."

The dragonets fluttered around my head.

"Thanks, guys."

They nodded their little heads, and we continued on, racing down the hall, our footsteps nearly silent.

"Almost there," Del whispered.

When the hall spilled into a large kitchen, I almost laughed in relief. We were so close.

The collapsed body of the cook and a guard were tied up and gagged near the stove. The cook, who I recognized by his dirty apron, shifted at the sound of our entrance. His gaze traveled to us, widening at the sight of our group. He thrashed, trying to send up the alert any way he could.

We ignored him, heading straight for a heavy wooden door.

"Don't touch the handle or it'll burn right through your hand," Aidan said.

He didn't need to tell me twice. I could feel the protection charm sparking against my skin from feet away. It felt like bee stings, and I wanted to swat at my skin to make them go away. It'd do no good, though.

Aidan stepped toward the door. "The protection charms on the door are too strong for my spell stripper. But we can get through one at a time with the Penatrist charms."

Thank magic we'd taken them from Victor's demons. A spell stripper would remove the protection from the door entirely, as long as it wasn't too strong. Penatrist charms were for the big guns, like this. They didn't remove the protection charm, but they'd allow one person through.

Aidan gave the charm he'd pulled out of his pocket to Emile, and I shoved mine into Claire's hand. "Go!"

Her brows shot up. "What about you?"

"No way I'm leaving first," I said. "Anyway, I can access some of my power, so it's best I stay behind in case guards show up. Now go!"

Emile and Claire gripped the charms in their hands and turned to the door. Claire grasped the handle and pulled it open, showing no sign of pain upon touching it.

It swung open easily, revealing a vast white tundra. I shivered. Claire and Emile stepped out, followed by the dragonets, who had no problem crossing the threshold without charms. On the other side, they disappeared, returning to wherever they had come from.

Claire turned around and thrust her hand back through the doorway. Emile did the same. Connor and Nix reached out and took the charms, both of them shuddering visibly when their hands neared the door.

But as soon as they took the Penatrist charms from Claire and Emile, they relaxed, no longer affected by the bee-stings of the door's protection charm.

They stepped through the doorway, into the tundra. As they were turning back to us, the sound of thundering footsteps reached my ears. The hair on my arms stood up.

"Guards are coming!" I said.

Connor and Nix thrust the charms back over the threshold. Del and Aidan grabbed them. Aidan pressed his into my hand, then shoved me through the door, not waiting for me to argue that he should go first.

I stumbled out into the cold, my feet aching at the feel of the icy stone step. I whirled around and thrust the charm back at Aidan, who grabbed it and lunged through just as guards streamed into the kitchen.

He slammed the door shut behind him, but it would only buy us seconds.

"I can transport two people," Del said as she grabbed Connor and Claire each by an arm.

"I've got a transportation charm." Aidan held out a small black stone. "Everyone else come with me."

We nodded. Del disappeared with Connor and Claire as Aidan threw the stone to the ground. A cloud of glittery gray smoke poofed up. We stepped in just as the door to the kitchen opened, revealing a horde of guards.

When I opened my eyes in my own living room, I almost fell over with relief. My heart was still pounding, but when the guards didn't show up, I knew they hadn't been able to follow us.

Home. It was tiny and cluttered, but it was all mine.

Everyone stood around me, tugging their masks off. I was so grateful to see everyone again, whole and hale. Last time I'd seen them, they'd been fleeing Victor and the bulldog. Del and Nix had been unconscious.

"You guys are the best! Thank you." I went in a circle, hugging everyone. "I was screwed right before you showed up."

"Thank magic for luck, then," Aidan said as he squeezed me hard. "The timing was coincidental. We'd just figured out where the prison was located. It's damned hard to find."

"Did you bring the dragonets?" I asked.

"No," Del said. "They showed up at the same time we did."

"I guess they're my guardian dragons." They'd shown up last time I'd really needed them, too, when I'd been facing off against Victor Orriodor at the stone circle near my parents' home. Thank magic, I wasn't going to look a gift dragon in the mouth.

"Are we safe here?" Emile asked. "Will they know to look for us?"

"They don't know my name," I said. "And my concealment charm works again. So they can't find me here. Do you have any kind of concealment charm that will block you from their seers, if they decide to look for you?"

Emile shook his head. "No."

"I can get you one." Aidan pulled out his phone and tapped a message in, then looked up. "Someone will be here in fifteen minutes to take care of it. And I've put the best protections available on this building."

"We haven't had any trouble the last few days," Nix said. "Any time Nix and I go out, we use a glamour charm to change our faces. That's all Dermot Mulvey could possibly recognize, because I don't think he knows our names either."

"Dermot Mulvey?" I asked.

"That big bastard from the Order of the Magica. Jowly fellow." Del gestured to her cheeks. "The one siding with Victor Orriodor."

"The bulldog. And yeah, he doesn't know your names," I said. "Which makes us safe for now, right?"

"As long as you use glamour charms when you're out and about in Magic's Bend, just in case you run into him," Aidan said.

So I had a reprieve. As long as I was careful, I could stay hidden from the Order and from Victor. They'd come for me, but this would give me time to prepare.

Relief made my knees weak. It was also probably hunger and adrenaline. I glanced over at Emile, who looked even skinnier and more ragged than he had back in the cell. Ralph and Rufus sat on his shoulders.

"Connor, can Emile borrow some of your clothes?" I asked. "And could you be a hero and bring some pasties over?" I had a sudden thought and glanced at Emile. "Are you a vegetarian?"

He nodded.

As I'd thought. If he could talk to animals, he probably didn't want to eat them.

"You can shower at my place," Del said. "Cass really needs to use her shower. Like, now."

I laughed. "Yeah, yeah." Though she was right. I'd never felt so grimy. "Let's meet back here in a bit. We've got a lot to talk about."

Aidan followed me to the shower. My bathroom was so tiny that he barely fit, but he managed. As soon as we got into the crowded space, he hugged me from behind.

I closed my eyes and leaned into him, then sighed, comfort flowing through every muscle and vein.

"That feels so good," I said.

"Does indeed."

"But I'm pretty gross."

He kissed the top my head. "Yeah, you are. But I don't mind. I'm just glad you're okay."

The relief in his voice was so palpable that I glanced into the mirror to see him. He towered over me, his broad shoulders filling the mirror over the sink. I was struck anew by how handsome he was, with his dark hair, gray eyes, and camping-model looks. Rugged, yet hot as hell. He could sell me a lantern and tent any day.

Then, I'd invite him inside.

But signs of his worry were visible as well. The shadows under his eyes were dark and his hair was mussed, like he'd been raking his hand through it. He even looked like he'd lost a little weight, though it'd been only three days.

But he'd recover. And so would I.

I turned around in his arms to face him. He leaned down and kissed me, his mouth warm and skilled on mine.

"I need a shower," I murmured against his lips.

"Don't care," he muttered. His big hands ran all over me, touching every bit that he could reach. "I was so damned worried. If something ever happened to you…"

He shook his head as if he couldn't even think of it, then took my mouth again. His kiss deepened, becoming possessive. Intense. Desperate. Like he was trying to make me part of him.

I shivered, losing myself in his touch. He smelled amazing—his evergreen magic, but also the scent of his skin and hair.

I couldn't get enough of him as I swept my hands over his broad shoulders and reveled in the taste of his lips. His tongue danced over mine, making my head spin.

A loud laugh from the living room broke through the bathroom door, the sound breaking my daze. Worry returned, creeping into my head. I pulled away. There were still so many questions.

"Is everyone really okay?" I asked. "You don't think the Order suspects you're involved with me? They don't know who Del and Nix are?"

He closed his eyes and shook his head as if to clear it, then met my gaze and said, "Haven't heard a peep from them. And I don't think they realize who or what you are. I've put feelers out, and I'm getting nothing back."

As I'd thought. "The bulldog—I mean, Dermot Mulvey—has something going on the side with Victor. That's why he hasn't squealed on me. Whatever they want us for, it's worth more than ratting me out and getting credit for catching a FireSoul."

"It's a reprieve for now, but I don't think it's a good thing."

"Definitely not. He's got something worse planned." I pulled out of his arms, then turned around and pressed a quick kiss to his lips. "But I can't think about it 'til I'm clean and fed."

"They didn't feed you well, I take it," he said as I turned on the shower.

"No. And I've been sharing with Ralph and Rufus for the last three days."

"I thought they looked plump."

I grinned. "Maybe. But they're good rats. I owe them, and Emile, a lot."

"I'll see that we help Emile find a new identity. The Order knows who and what he is. He'll need help staying under their radar."

"You're the best, you know that?"

He inclined his head, not entirely modestly.

I grinned, then made shooing motions. "Scram. I need some alone time. But I want a rain check on what we started earlier."

"All yours." He winked, then stepped out.

Quickly, I shucked my clothes and climbed into my tiny shower. The tiles were cracked and dingy and the whole thing was about the size of a slice of toast, but no shower had ever felt as good. Not even a shower in Aidan's masterpiece of a bathroom at his house in Ireland.

When the door cracked open, I called, "Who is it?"

"Special delivery!" Nix's voice rang out. A hand clutching a can of Pabst Blue Ribbon shoved into the shower.

"Oh, thank magic, you're the best," I said as I took the icy can. It may be the beer of hipsters and hillbillies, but they had good taste, because it was my beer of choice, too. I didn't care that it was only one step up from water in the estimation of beer snobs.

"It was my idea," Del said.

I gulped down the chilly beer, grateful to taste anything that wasn't gruel or stale water.

"I'm so glad you guys are all right," I said as I set the beer on the tiny shelf. My shampoo clattered to the ground, but I ignored it. I was already clean.

"Thanks to you," Del said.

"Yeah, I heard you pulled some heroic, self-sacrificing shit," Nix said.

"Shit?" I slammed off the water, annoyed.

A towel landed on my head. One of them must have tossed it over the rail. I wrapped it around myself, then yanked open the curtain. "Did you just call my rescue *shit*?"

"Yeah, you idiot," Nix said. "You could have gotten killed. Don't pull that kind of crap again."

"I had to save you." I wanted to kick her.

"I know." Nix hugged me, squeezing hard enough to force all the air from my lungs. But it was a stiff hug, and her voice was stilted. "You took a dumb risk. You could've been killed."

Nix scooted back, and Del came in for her own hug, then pinched me hard on the butt. I yelped as she pulled away.

"Why the hell did you do it?" Del's blue eyes glinted angrily. "You left yourself with no backup."

I shrugged, suddenly uncomfortable. I didn't usually make stupid moves like that, but it'd been necessary. "You were unconscious. It was the only way to get you out of there. I knew it was a risk, but I don't... I don't want to be in a world without you."

"Yeah, well, it's kinda mutual, dummy." Del hugged me hard again. "Thank you. But next time, don't risk yourself like that."

Del stepped back, and I could see Nix crowded into the corner of the small bathroom. Her eyes glinted with angry tears. She'd worked herself into a good rage. She was the slow burner of our group.

"We were so worried about you," Nix said. "I woke up from that sleeping potion, and no one knew what had happened to you. We couldn't find you for days."

I could understand their anger. If they'd taken such a dumb freaking risk to save me, I'd be pissed too. I'd gotten ridiculously lucky at the Prison for Magical Miscreants, and I knew it. Something terrible could have happened to me there. If I were in their position? I'd rather die than wake up knowing they'd been killed trying to save me.

Nothing was simple, was it?

I squeezed past Del and hugged Nix, who stiffened.

"I love you, Nix. I'm really sorry," I said.

She relaxed slowly. "I know. And thank you. It was a huge thing you did, holding off Dermot Mulvey and his guards. But don't do it again. I don't want to lose you."

I hugged her tighter, not speaking my fear—that we all might lose each other if Victor Orriodor got his hands on us.

# CHAPTER THREE

"I come bearing gifts!" Connor held up big paper bags as he entered my apartment ten minutes later. The smell of spiced beef and buttery pastry wafted from inside, and my stomach growled.

"What would I do without you?" I grinned as he handed me a Cornish Pasty. Connor and Claire were from England, a fact I was thankful for every time I ate one of their delicious pasties. The savory treats were a hit at their coffee shop, Potions & Pastilles.

I scarfed down my food while sitting on the couch, grateful to be wearing my own clothes. Jeans and a t-shirt had never felt so good. I wanted to burn that old prison jumpsuit.

Aidan and my *deirfiúr* knew better than to try to talk to me at this particular second. I wasn't going to stop chewing until I was full. Emile changed into some of Connor's clothes—his standard skinny jeans and a band t-shirt. He'd found a seat on my old lounge chair and ate his potato and veggie pasty with relish.

Ralph and Rufus split one of their own, both of them sitting on a plate on the coffee table. My friends were scattered on the couch and in chairs they'd pulled in from my tiny dining nook.

Altogether, it would have been a homey scene if we weren't being hunted by a sociopath.

I polished off the last bite of pasty, then looked up. "Okay. We need to figure out what Victor Orriodor is up to."

Nix tucked her dark hair behind her ear, then held up her hand and began ticking things off. "Well, he's collecting powerful magical objects to help with his end goal. He wants vengeance against someone, and he wants to use us to get it."

That about summed it up. Three big things that could lead to disaster. We'd recently learned that Del, Nix, and I formed the Triumvirate, a trio of prophesied supernaturals who represented the balance between life, death, and magic. Nix was life, Del was Death, and I was magic.

I didn't know what the hell it all meant, but we were trying to figure it out.

"I think I can help you with that," Emile said.

Everyone turned to look at him.

"Yeah?" I asked. "Does this have anything to do with how the Alpha Council figured out you were a FireSoul and imprisoned you?"

He nodded. "Victor Orriodor got to me first, though. He wanted me to help him break into the Alpha Council headquarters. My animals can act as the perfect spies. They can even trip levers to break into places. Open doors and gates, that kind of thing."

"Why did he want to get into Glencarrough?" I asked, though I thought I knew.

"To help him steal the Heartstone and Heart of Glencarrough."

I nodded slowly. It made sense. The Heartstone was a magical artifact that provided protection to whoever possessed it. The Heart of Glencarrough was the person assigned to tend to it—it was always a child, pure of heart. A month ago, the Alpha Council had hired me to retrieve the two when they had been stolen. We'd saved the child, but not the Heartstone.

"So you did it?" Nix asked.

"He threatened me. He was going to put a slave collar on me, but it interfered with my ability to speak to my animals. So he had to take it off. I agreed to help him so that I could alert the Alpha Council to what he was trying. But when I went to them, they didn't listen. They tossed me in the dungeon instead for being a FireSoul."

"And that's what hate and ignorance will get you," Del said. "Idiot Shifters."

"But Victor got in anyway?" I asked.

"Yes. I didn't use my animals to help him, but I think he took advantage of the furor over what I was. The Alpha Council was busy freaking out over me, and he slipped in and took what he wanted."

"So, do you think he wants vengeance on the Alpha Council?" I asked. "We originally thought he wanted the Heartstone and Heart of Glencarrough to protect something of his own."

Emile shrugged. "That could be it, but his castle is very heavily fortified. The mountains around it are nearly impassable. I don't know if he'd even need anything more to defend it. So I think he was trying to weaken the Alpha Council's defenses."

"Castle?" Nix asked. "What do you mean, castle? I thought he lived in a mansion at a waypoint. It's in the middle of a desert."

Emile shook his head. "I never went there. I met with him at a castle in some mountains, though I don't know which because I was blindfolded during the travel."

"So he's got two headquarters." I leaned back against the couch. "That may be where he's hiding the other FireSouls he's kidnapped."

Victor hunted and enslaved FireSouls to help him with his end goals. Often, they were children.

"Makes sense," Del said. "There were none in his dungeon at the waypoint last month. And he knows he's constantly hunted—by us and any adult FireSouls he's enslaved who might want to kill him. I'd have two hidey-holes if I were him, too."

"Okay, great," I said. "So we'll file that away as one more thing to address."

If Victor had FireSouls locked up in some creepy castle—especially *child* FireSouls—I was going to get them the hell out. But first we needed to find them.

"So Victor may want vengeance on the Alpha Council, and he's planning something big," Aidan said. "Big enough that he needed to knock out their defenses to make it happen."

"Could be," Emile said.

"The Alpha Council said they could create a new Heartstone to protect Glencarrough," I said, thinking back to the conversation I'd had with Elenora, their leader. "But they said it would take a while. It's been over a month. I wonder how they're coming along?"

"We can go warn them," Del said.

"Yeah, we could." I nodded. "But we aren't even sure if that's his goal. We need more info. Let's find this Dermot Mulvey. Ask him some questions. If a member of the Order of the Magica is involved with this, we want to know what he's up to so we can tell the Alpha Council."

"That's not going to be easy," Aidan said. "I've heard that Mulvey's home is well protected."

I grinned. "Good thing we're used to breaking into places, then, isn't it?"

"It's smaller than I expected." I examined Dermot Mulvey's house from the cover of the trees. "And so average."

Dermot Mulvey didn't actually live in Magic's Bend, Aidan had learned. He kept a house outside of Portland, a city largely inhabited by humans. On the surface, it was an odd move for an Order member. But it made sense for a guy who was going behind the Order's back with Victor Orriodor.

His house, on the other hand, was a definite surprise. It sat in the middle of a clearing in the woods. Sunlight shined on the two-story brick building that looked like it only had four bedrooms, max. For most people, it'd be a good size house. Big, even.

For Dermot Mulvey, whose office took up nearly an entire floor of the tallest building in Magic's Bend, it was weird. He was definitely someone who liked to throw wealth around. This house didn't follow that pattern, though. And Aidan's security colleague who'd done the work on it had said it was hard to get into.

But this didn't look so bad.

After a good night's sleep—during which Aidan had kept me company—we made the two-hour drive to the bulldog's house. This was supposed to be a stealth operation, so everyone else had stayed behind.

Our goal was to sneak in, get the bulldog alone, and dose him with the truth serum. Del and Nix had wanted to come, but we'd all agreed that if we were caught, we shouldn't be together. Victor needed all three of us for his plans, and we didn't want to make it easy for him.

"Looks like there are only two guards," Aidan murmured.

The massive men stood on either side of the front door, black suit jackets too tight in the shoulders and open at the waist. To allow access to a weapon? We were too far away to get a feel for their magical signature, so I didn't know what they were capable of.

I fiddled with the small vial of truth serum that Connor had whipped up for us in his secondary kitchen—the one specifically for potion making. Then I tucked it deep into the small bag slung over my back and grabbed the potion bomb full of sleeping potion.

I still had my magic and my daggers, but the magic was usually loud and the daggers were deadly. I didn't want to attract attention, and I didn't want to kill the bulldog's guards. They were probably just some schmucks hired by the Magica.

"Remember, no killing," I said. I was more than willing to eviscerate Victor Orriodor and even the bulldog, but not his guards. Not unless they had their hands around my throat. "Not unless there's no other way."

He nodded, though he looked a bit grumpy. He agreed with me on principle, but with my life at risk, he didn't want to take any chances.

Now that I had such a massive amount of power running through my veins, it made me more wary of actually using it. Just because I could blast a whole bunch of guys into oblivion didn't mean I *should*.

I wore the golden dampening charm around my wrist because I didn't have full control of my power yet, so I was free to operate as normal. But I could take it off any time and blow things to hell.

I wanted to avoid that. At least until I had a chance to practice.

"Let's get a move on," I said. "I'll take the guy on the left."

Aidan dug a potion bomb out of his pocket and grinned at me. "Then I'll take the fellow on the right."

The morning was clear and bright, with nary a shadow for cover. Fortunately, we were able to hide in the woods.

"On three," I said.

Aidan nodded, and I counted. When I hit three, we hurled our bombs. I was a good shot from all my dagger practice, and my potion bomb exploded on the guard's burly chest half a second before Aidan's bomb hit the other guard in the shoulder. Sparkling green liquid exploded over them, and they both stiffened. Their eyes rolled up in their heads, and they toppled forward.

"Good shot," I said.

"Not as good as yours."

"No." I grinned. "Come on."

We raced across the grass toward the house. I shivered when the prickly sense of the house's protection charm hit me. Ugh. I hated that feeling.

When we reached the fallen guards, I pulled a few strips of heavy rope and two gags from my bag and handed some to Aidan.

Quickly, we bound and gagged the guards, just in case they woke up earlier than anticipated. Up close, I could smell Shifter. These weren't the same guards as he'd brought to the prison. Those had been Magica. These guys were some kind of Shifter—probably predators. Big ones.

I dusted off my hands and stood, then nodded at Aidan. He grinned, then pulled a small silver charm from his pocket. I'd seen him use the Spell Stripper before, but I was struck anew with jealousy. It was a handy little device that would go a long way in my treasure hunting endeavors, allowing me to get past charms that would take me longer to figure out.

I grinned. I should ask for one for my birthday.

Aidan ran the charm over the boundaries of the door. The prickly magic of the protection charm slowly faded, and I breathed a sigh of relief. Protection charms usually felt awful, but that one had been worse. Like hundreds of little bee stings.

"We're in," Aidan murmured, then pushed open the door.

I followed him into a small foyer, struck by how quiet the place was. And it smelled weird.... Abandoned, almost. Like dust and a bit of mold.

"Not home?" I mouthed at Aidan.

He frowned and shook his head. One of his many contacts had reported that the bulldog had returned home yesterday evening after his failed attempt to question me at the prison. So he should be here. There was even a big black SUV in the drive.

I gestured for Aidan to follow me and crept toward the arched exit that led to another room. It turned out to be the kitchen, but this room was even weirder than the foyer.

"Fake food?" I stared at the plastic breakfast that had been set out on the table—cereal and milk along with half a cup of coffee. But up close, it was obviously not real.

"He doesn't live here," Aidan said.

"It's a false front." I glanced at the window. "From the window, it would look real."

"And the guards were real," Aidan said. "If he just has this place for show, they could have been illusion. But he's choosing to pay real people to protect this place."

I looked around, now fully convinced that no one lived here. It looked like a model home, with a thin veneer of habitation—the fake food, fake plants, and a pile of bills that were no doubt also not real.

"Let's look around," I said. "Something's off."

We made our way around the house on silent feet. Every room was just like the kitchen—scattered with the detritus of everyday life, but carefully staged. A wooden door under the stairs caught my eye.

"Basement next?" I asked.

Aidan went to the door and pulled on the handle, but it didn't budge. He withdrew his hand and shook it, as if burned.

"I guess it's not just locked," I said.

"No. There are protections on it."

"We're onto something, then."

Aidan pulled the spell stripper out of his pocket again and killed the protection charms on the door. This time when he tried to open it, it did easily.

He led the way down the darkened staircase.

A slight shuffling sound in the darkness was my only warning.

"Down!" I yelled as I dug into my bag for a potion bomb.

Aidan ducked as I raised my hand, igniting my lightstone ring. It blazed in the dark, illuminating an ordinary basement with a very unordinary giant scorpion lurking in the dark.

*Shit.* I hurled the potion bomb, praying to magic as it splattered against his terrifying face. Brilliant green goo dripped off his fangs, but the creature barely tottered on its spindly legs, so I dug out another and hurled it. This time, the monster swayed. When Aidan hit it with one of his bombs, the scorpion crashed to the ground.

"Holy hell," Aidan muttered. "Didn't expect that."

"Nope." I patted my bag, dismayed to feel only one more potion bomb.

"I think we're onto something, though," Aidan said.

"Yep." I glanced around the room, noticing the scorpion's signs of habitation. A weird nest and a rotting smell. "But what was he doing down here? Guarding something?"

Aidan walked to the wall that the scorpion had been standing near and ran his fingertips along it. "There may be a hidden door."

"Smart." I joined him, training my fingers along the dusty wall. "This house is just the entrance to his real home. He could invite guests here. Reporters would think they had a real address, and if they looked in the windows, they'd just think he was gone."

"But the scorpion guards the passage to his real residence."

My fingertips buzzed with electric magic when they passed over a certain part of the wall. "Think I found it."

I stepped back and stared at the wall, unable to see the door. Aidan joined me and pulled his spell stripper from his pocket, then ran it along the wall. A long vertical line began to glow. At about seven feet high, it took a right turn. After a few feet, it turned again and headed down to the floor. Outlining a door. A moment later, the concealment charm faded, and the actual door appeared.

"Nice work." I pushed it open and peered into the darkened corridor. It was tiled in black granite, with modern light fixtures hanging from the ceiling every twenty feet. They looked expensive. In fact, the whole place was a complete 180 from the boring house and dingy basement. "This is more the bulldog's taste."

Aidan stepped in behind me. "Yes. Much more his style."

We made our way silently down the hall. My muscles were tense and my ears perked, but there was only silence. Would the house at the other end be underground, like some weird mole person's home? Or perhaps it'd be hidden from the outside world by illusion.

I was so distracted by the thought that I almost didn't hear the strange slithering, rattling sound coming from beneath our feet.

"Stop!" I grabbed the back of Aidan's shirt and jerked him to a halt.

He stopped abruptly, his big form dead-still. "What is it?"

I strained my ears and sniffed the air. A strange, dry scent hit my nose, totally unidentifiable. But the slithering sound wasn't. "I think it's... snakes."

"Snakes? I can't hear them." He looked at me quizzically. "How can you?"

"My hearing has been crazy good ever since I unlocked my root power. I don't know why."

His brow creased. "It's probably enhancing the Shifter power that you took from Victor's pet wolf."

I hadn't thought about that. Victor's pet wolf had been one of two female wolf Shifters who'd worked for him. They'd abducted a little girl and tried to kill me. So when I'd had a chance to take one of the wolves' Shifter power, I hadn't hesitated. I'd known I'd need every skill I could get in order to defeat Victor, and she'd been a second away from killing me. In hindsight, I felt weirdly guilty about it all, but now wasn't the time to examine that.

"Makes sense." I studied the floor and walls. "I think there's a booby-trap here."

"That's very paranoid of Dermot. Though the giant scorpion set the tone for paranoid, I'd say."

"Yeah. And very old school." As in, Egyptian pyramid old school. I reached out to Aidan. "Hold my hand."

His big palm gripped mine. I squeezed it tight, then poked my toe forward, feeling my way along the marble floor, trying to trip the booby-trap to find out where it was. I moved cautiously. Though Aidan would keep me from plummeting in, I didn't want to chance it. I'd dangled over a pit of creepy crawlies a few times in my career, and I didn't want a repeat.

When the floor tile disappeared out from under my toe, I leapt back, my heart pounding.

"Found it." I let go of Aidan's hand and moved forward, peering into the pit that had opened in the floor. About ten feet down, black snakes writhed within.

"Thank magic for your new hearing," Aidan muttered. "Wouldn't want to fall into that."

Though it was deep, it was only about five feet across. "I think we can jump it."

Aidan nodded. We stepped back to take a running start, then leapt over the hole one at a time. It was a close call for me, but I made it with inches to spare. We set off down the hall again, more cautious than before.

We'd gone a long way with no more traps—perhaps as far as a quarter mile—by the time a door appeared at the other end.

Unfortunately, a guard appeared with it. His mouth opened to shout just as Aidan hurled a potion bomb at him. It exploded against his chest, the glass shattering and the liquid soaking him. A moment later, his eyes rolled up in his head, and he passed out. His massive form tumbled to the ground.

"Connor's potions really are handy," I whispered. "I ought to use them more often."

"Hopefully you won't need them after we figure this thing out."

"True." I wanted to get back to my normal life. One of tomb raiding and friends and hanging out. In my normal life, I didn't need potion bombs loaded with sleeping spells because I just killed the demons who got in my way. I didn't have to deal with humans. But the only way out was forward.

We nodded at each other as a signal to go, then crept silently down the hall. When we reached the end, I pushed the door slowly. It creaked open, revealing a set of stairs leading up.

So the house was above ground.

"Looks like he probably has his real house hidden by illusion, because I don't think I saw any houses around his dummy house," I said.

Aidan nodded and we began to climb. At the top, I nudged open the heavy wooden door and peered into a foyer. It was a grand place, all shining dark wood lit by a crystal chandelier above. The chandelier sent glittering sparkles of light on the floor.

"Bingo." This was truly the bulldog's house—and it was one of his mistakes. No one would believe that he lived in that modest family dwelling we'd just been in.

I stood in the doorway, trying to figure out if anyone was home. There was only silence in the house. I strained my ears, listening for music or footsteps or talking.

"I think I hear something to the left," I whispered.

Aidan cocked his head, then jerked it toward the right. "Agreed."

We crept out of the doorway and through the foyer, then down the wide hallway dotted with oil paintings. I suppressed a shudder at the memory of escaping Victor Orriodor's compound as a child. His home had been just as ornate as this, with terrors down below in the basement. What was Dermot Mulvey hiding?

We found him in an office, leaned back in a chair with his feet propped up on the desk. He was dressed in one of his usual snappy suits and chatting into his phone, looking like the overinflated criminal blowhard that he was.

Then again, maybe I was biased.

Okay, I was definitely biased. I hated this bastard and wanted to figure out what the hell he was doing with scum like Victor Orriodor.

He faced away from the door, so we had a second before he saw us. I nodded at Aidan and we charged, each taking a side. Dermot heard us coming and surged to his feet, spinning to face us, his eyes wide.

He threw up his hands, no doubt to cast a protective shield around himself, but I leapt on him before he could. We crashed to the ground, and I scrambled on top.

"You!" he spat.

"Yep." I grinned, then jumped off him as Aidan crouched and grabbed Dermot's shoulders, yanking him up.

Quickly, Aidan tugged Dermot's hands behind his back, snapping on a pair of silver handcuffs that we'd brought along for that very purpose.

"We have some questions," I said as Aidan directed him to a chair.

"And you presume that I will answer them?" Dermot blustered.

I sat on his desk, propping my boot on a drawer handle. I was really enjoying the power switch. This bastard had threatened my *deirfiúr* and tossed me in prison.

I grinned at Dermot, then pulled one of my obsidian blades from the sheath at my thigh. His eyes widened before his jaw hardened.

"Steeling yourself for torture?" I asked. Frankly, I didn't have the stomach for it, but he didn't know that.

"That's what you'd do in this situation, isn't it? That's what you intended when you came to my cell at the Prison for Magical Miscreants."

I flipped the blade up into the air, enjoying the way the light glimmered on the black glass. I also enjoyed the way Dermot swallowed hard, fear in his beady eyes. I might not have the stomach for torture, but I was no saint. I enjoyed his fear.

"It is what you had planned," I answered for him. "Fortunately for you, I have a friend who is uncommonly good with potions. One of the best in the world, in fact."

I pulled a little vile from my pocket and nodded at Aidan. He grabbed Dermot's head, tilting it back. Dermot thrashed, but Aidan pinched his nose, forcing him to open his mouth. I tugged the cork out of the vial and poured the black liquid into Dermot's mouth. Aidan pushed on Dermot's jaw, forcing him to swallow.

"There now," I said, knowing I was being insufferable. "That's not so bad, is it?"

Dermot shot daggers at me with his eyes and strained against Aidan's hold. Our plan had been to have Aidan guard the door, but none of the furniture in here was sturdy enough to tie Dermot to, and he definitely wasn't going to sit still.

"So," I said. "Those questions I have. Let's get started. What are Victor Orriodor's plans?"

Dermot's gaze darted left and right. Sweat rolled down his forehead. According to Connor, the potion would compel Dermot to answer my questions. He was fighting it now, but he couldn't hold out forever.

"Dermot?" I nudged his knee with my boot.

"To destroy the Alpha Council." His complexion turned green as soon as he spat out the words.

As I'd thought. "Why?"

"Vengeance. For his family."

That was fair enough. I'd seen in a vision from the past that a group of armed men had killed his parents for being FireSouls. I couldn't blame Victor, though I didn't think he should murder a bunch of people.

"Have you told the Order of the Magica about Cass being a FireSoul?" Aidan asked.

I glared at him. I was asking the questions here. But Aidan glared right back at me. His priority was my safety. It always had been. Though I wanted other answers more, Aidan seemed determined to get his in.

"No," Dermot bit out.

Relief loosened a couple of the knots in my shoulders. My secret was still safe. I hadn't realized how much I'd wanted confirmation on that point.

We'd probably have to kill Dermot to keep my secret, a task I didn't relish. With my new strength, there were no more even fights. It made me hate the idea of killing even more than I had before. I had too much power. But as long as I focused on the threat he posed to my *deirfiúr*, I could do what I had to.

"Why?" Aidan asked.

"We need her and the other two. If the Order knew what she was, she'd stay locked up in the prison where we couldn't get her."

"Then why put her there in the first place?"

"I needed someplace to hold her while I settled things after the disaster at my office. There was an inquiry. Too many questions." He scowled. "I couldn't have her under foot, and I had a contact at the prison. I needed a few days to deal with the fall-out, and it was the only place strong enough to hold her."

"And it failed, didn't it?" I grinned.

"Yes," he growled.

I reveled in his frustration, but I was starting to feel some of it myself. He was confirming my suspicions, but I wanted new info. "Is Victor planning to use the Heartstone to break into Glencarrough? Or does he want it to protect his stronghold?"

"He's going to use it against Glencarrough. His stronghold is secure."

"Where is it?"

"A castle in the mountains of Transylvania."

I barked a laugh. "You're kidding."

"No."

"Really? He's got a creepy castle in Transylvania. Like Dracula."

He nodded his head sharply.

"Of course he does." I shook my head. Victor was the scariest man I'd ever met. This should humanize him. Make him seem slightly ridiculous. But I had a feeling that if I saw that castle, he'd still be just as scary. "Are there FireSoul prisoners there? Children?"

"I'm not sure."

"But you think there might be."

"There might."

Damn. "Where is this place, exactly?"

"In the middle of Romania, bordered on the east and south by the Carpathian Mountains. The castle is in the heart of the mountains. At the tallest peak."

I pulled out my phone and found the maps app, then pulled up Transylvania. It was small, a weird-shaped region in the middle of Romania. I found the mountains and zoomed in, looking for the tallest peak according to the topography markers. I dropped a pin in it and held the phone out so that Dermot could see.

"Is that where it is?"

"Roughly."

I nodded. We'd find it. "How is Victor planning to take down the Alpha Council? And why do you want him to?"

Dermot's eyes shifted around the room. Like he was looking for an escape. Or help. Were there more guards?

Probably.

"Well?" I poked his knee with my boot.

"He's going to waken something greater and more powerful than he is. An ancient force that he'll use to fuel himself with more power. Enough to accomplish *all* his goals."

*Oooh, shit.* A greater power? In the case of Victor, that had to mean a greater, more *evil* power. I thought I'd already seen the worst, but he thought there was more?

"How?" I demanded.

"I don't know."

"Yes, you do. Tell me." I wanted to shake him. Victor already had more power than any supernatural I'd ever met. Even me. I might have recently gained my endless well of power, but I couldn't control it. He could.

If Victor was already so powerful, what was stronger than him? What was worse than him?

Goosebumps broke out over my arms.

"Tell me, damn it." I held my dagger at his throat, hoping to scare him into talking.

"I'm not sure how he plans to get it!" Dermot cried.

He'd taken the truth serum, so I had to believe him. "What do you get out of all this?"

His gaze darted shiftily around the room.

"Tell me!"

"He'll give me some of the power," he said. "Enough that I'll be the second strongest Magica. Behind him."

What a pipe dream. Victor wouldn't share shit.

"What do you give him in exchange?" Aidan asked.

"Money and men and—"

The room exploded with action and shattered glass. Men burst in through the windows behind Dermot's chair. Four of them, all dressed in black tactical gear.

"Behind you!" Aidan shouted.

I spun to see six people surging into the room. Their magical signatures filled the air, the crackle of fire and the cold burn of ice. There were at least a few Elemental Mages in the bunch, but probably some other nasties as well.

*Shit.* Dermot must have managed to hit a panic button.

Beside me, a glow of gray light suffused Aidan. A second later, the massive griffin stood in his place. His golden fur and feathers reflected the light, and his massive beak snapped threateningly.

"Try not to kill them," I muttered, my new conscience getting the better of me.

Aidan glared at me, then turned to charge the guards climbing through the windows. I hoped he'd just head-butt them or something.

I called upon my magic, going for my Mirror Mage powers. I was pissed enough that I wanted to use Dermot's own weather witch powers to defeat him.

The guards on the other side of the room threw jets of flame and spears of ice at me. Heat and gold flew by me as I dodged. I lunged behind Dermot's desk as I reached out for his magic. He sneered down at me from the chair above.

I grinned at him as I caught hold of the gusting wind that was part of his weather witch gift, then rolled out from behind the desk and threw a massive blast of wind at the two nearest guards. They flew backward and slammed into the wall.

Out of nowhere, a jet of ice hit me right in the stomach, bowling me backward. Pain exploded from my middle, stealing my breath. Aching, I scrambled upright. I hadn't even seen it coming.

Across the room, a Fire Mage held a glowing ball of flame in his hand. He hurled it at me. As it flew through the air, it grew in size and shape. I threw out my hand and sent a gust of wind at the fireball. The flame surged back toward its master, dissipating as it flew. My torrent of air had extinguished most of it by the time it crashed into the Fire Mage's chest. He slammed into the wall, but at least he wasn't devoured by the flame.

These guys were playing for keeps. Whatever button Dermot had pressed, it'd been the serious one. I'd knocked out three of the guards who'd come through the door, but there were still five left.

Aidan's roar echoed in the room, making my ears ache. I glanced quickly behind me. He'd knocked out four guards, but more climbed through the window. Half a dozen on his side of the room, and they were rushing toward him. He was seriously handicapped by my request that he not kill.

We were outnumbered.

*Shit, shit, shit.*

I'd gotten cocky, questioning Dermot. Now, we'd be lucky to make it out of here at all. I turned back to my side of the room and gave it one more shot.

As soon as I turned, a massive spear of ice hurtled toward me. I lunged to the side and threw a blast of wind at the Magica who'd thrown it. She went flying backward, slamming into the wall. I tried heaving more blasts at the other guards, but I wasn't fast enough.

I needed my root power if I was going to get out of this.

But it was dangerous.

So was getting caught. I wouldn't escape the Prison for Magical Miscreants twice. Worse, I couldn't let Aidan be captured.

There was only one way.

I lunged to my feet and raced across the room to Aidan, dodging blasts of flame and ice that tore apart the room. Wood splinters and crystal shattered all around me.

When I reached Aidan, I leapt upon his back and jerked off the golden dampener cuff. Magic roared through me, making my hair stand on end. I gasped. *Whoa.*

"Fold in your wings!" I yelled. I couldn't guarantee I wouldn't hit Aidan with my magic, but as long as he was close to me, it was far less likely. He often used his wings to protect me. But that wouldn't help now.

The magic roiled within me, desperate to be set free. I'd have to try something non-deadly, not only to soothe my conscience, but to guarantee that Aidan wouldn't get killed in the blowback.

I called upon Dermot's weather witch power, hoping wind would do the trick. What had previously felt like a warm summer breeze now felt like a tornado raring to be set free. It roared within me, pounding to get out. I threw out both arms and envisioned a wave of wind bowling over my enemies.

The gust burst forth, roaring out of me in all directions. It up-ended all the furniture and people, slamming everything and everybody into the walls. Then the walls in the room collapsed. And then more walls as every wall in the house blew away. The noise was thunderous.

Aidan stumbled to his knees beneath me, but remained upright. I looked up, wondering why the ceiling hadn't fallen on us.

Above me, the roof was flying into the blue sky, propelled by the wind I'd produced. I'd created a dome of wind, blowing everything up and out.

"Holy shit," I breathed.

The roof overhead grew larger.

Shit! It was now falling back to earth. The wind had died.

"Aidan! Go!"

He staggered to his feet and took off, his massive wings carrying us away from the house. His powerful body surged beneath mine as he hurled us into the air.

Dermot's house had been in a forest. There were no other buildings nearby. We were in the trees when a loud crash echoed through the woods. I spun to look.

The roof had fallen back onto the house. My insides clenched as the black tar of guilt washed over me.

*I'd killed all those people.* They didn't necessarily know they were working for someone evil.

And I'd killed them. My skin grew cold and my stomach sour. Hot tears prickled my eyes. Had I really done it? Killed all those people?

I couldn't look away from Dermot's house as it grew smaller in the distance. The massive pile of mangled stone and wood that we left behind was a horrible visual of the carnage I was capable of. I shuddered.

I really needed to get control of my power. Because if I didn't control it, my magic could be as dark as Victor's.

# CHAPTER FOUR

I clung to Aidan's back, my mind racing, for the entirety of the ride back to Magic's Bend. The wind was cold enough to chill my bones, but I barely felt it.

When we landed on the wide expanse of his green backyard, I stumbled to the ground. Aidan's house was located at the edge of Enchanter's Bluff, the nicest neighborhood in town. He owned a big plot of land that butted up to the ocean, and I could hear the waves crashing against the rocky shore. I sucked in a deep breath of the fresh sea air and tried to clear my head.

Gray light swirled around the massive griffin who watched me with concerned eyes. A moment later, Aidan stood in its place, looking as calm and put-together as usual. No matter what kind of fight we were in, he usually ended up looking like he'd just stepped out of a catalogue.

"Are you all right?" He pulled me into his arms.

I melted into him, thawed by his heat. For just a second, I let his strength support me. We'd only been together for a couple of months, and none of it had been normal, but I couldn't imagine my life without him.

"Cass? You okay?" His breath was warm against the top of my head.

"No," I mumbled. Images of the blown-apart house flashed in my mind. *I'd* done that? I'd just meant to blow folks over. Stun them a bit so we could make our escape. Instead, I'd...

"I killed all those people," I murmured. My stomach still felt like it'd been dipped in acid, and my tears had dehydrated me totally. There were none left. "There were so many of them, and I killed them."

"You don't know that."

I looked up at him. "Come on, Aidan, of course I do. Did you see that? A house fell on them."

He gripped my shoulders. "You didn't mean to. You were defending yourself."

"I know. But tell that to their families." I shook my head, trying to banish the image of the crushed house. *I'm turning into a monster.* "I have so much power that I could have ended that all without death. But I can't control it. I never should have used it. That was so careless of me."

I clenched my fists in his shirtfront. This much power was a problem. A huge problem.

I looked down at my hands. "It's just that this new power I have... It makes me so much stronger than everyone else. I'm so aware of it now. It was one thing when it was an even fight and I was scrapping for my life. But now, it's just unfair. I can blast people away with a thought."

Understanding lit his gray eyes. "It's understandable that it makes you nervous."

"I just feel like I'm finally growing a conscience."

He grinned. "You've always had a conscience. You've just valued protecting your *deirfiúr* over anything else."

"Yeah."

"Just because you are now stronger doesn't mean you aren't at risk. That your *deirfiúr* aren't at risk."

"You're right. I need to get my head in the game. I guess I spent too much time mulling things over in prison."

He pulled me toward him and hugged me tight. "I think it's good you're taking your power into account. Becoming more responsible. But don't forget to protect yourself. I admire your honorable heart, but you can't let it paralyze you."

"I won't."

He stepped away. "But you do need to practice your magic."

I nodded vehemently. "God, I hope I can master it."

"You'll learn and become more comfortable. In the meantime, I'll send men to check on the house. To see about survivors. Maybe they survived."

I knew they hadn't, but I appreciated it. "Thank you."

He kissed me again, then pulled his phone out of his pocket. As he made the call, I realized he hadn't worn a mask to see Dermot. Until now, Dermot hadn't known he was involved.

He hung up the phone, and I said, "You didn't wear a mask."

"No." He shrugged.

Understanding dawned. "You weren't planning to let him live."

He gave me a look like I was crazy. "He threw you in the Prison for Magical Miscreants. He plans to use you in some horrible plot. Of course I wouldn't let him live. Neither would you, I don't think, no matter how you're feeling about your new power."

I nodded slowly. "You're right. I wouldn't have killed his men, but I'd have made myself kill him to protect my *deirfiúr*."

"It would have been the right thing to do."

I knew he was right, but I didn't want to think about it. I tugged my phone out of my pocket and glanced at the time. It was three o'clock. "We're going to need to alert the Alpha Council soon, but I want to know more about this greater power that Victor is seeking. That sounds really bad."

Aidan scrubbed a hand over his face, his gaze worried. "I agree. Whatever he's seeking, we can't let him get it. And we need to know more about his Transylvanian castle. If we're going to rescue any FireSouls, we'll need more details abut the castle's defenses. Going in blind is a death wish."

"We could ask Aethelred to scry for us." Aethelred was the only seer who I knew personally. He wasn't always a fan of me, but he'd help.

"Good idea," Aidan said.

"I'm going to call him. If he's in Darklane, I can head over there now. You can call the Alpha Council and tell them what's up."

"We have no evidence of Dermot Mulvey's betrayal or Victor's intentions, so I'm going to have to talk to the Alpha Council in person and hope they believe me," Aidan said. "And now that Dermot is dead, it's going to be even harder."

"Good point." Accusations should be made in person. That way, they'd at least take the claim seriously. Just calling up on the phone and naming names was suspicious.

But it was too dangerous for me to go with him when they could possibly sense what I was. I'd gone to their stronghold twice before, and both times had been risky as hell. I couldn't go back. Mathias, the one Shifter who knew what I was, had made that clear.

"Call Aethelred," Aidan said. "I'll go with you to Darklane, then I'll head to Scotland to meet with the Alpha Council."

"Good plan. While you're there, I'll practice my magic."

Aidan glanced around. "You shouldn't practice here."

"Oh, right. Sorry." I looked around at the big, beautifully manicured lawn. The house sat on the grass back from the sea, edged on both sides by trees. I'd blow this place right up.

"I'm not worried about the house," Aidan said. "But we're too close to the city. Dermot's home was hidden by illusion, so hopefully that concealed most of the blast.

But here, someone could see. If you thought folks were scared of you when you were a FireSoul, that's nothing compared to how they would feel if they knew what you can do now."

I blanched. "Good point."

"You can practice on my land in Scotland. It's near the Alpha Council headquarters."

"All right. I'll call Aethelred, then we'll head to Scotland."

Fortunately, Aethelred was home when I called. He agreed to meet with us in exchange for a bag of Connor's famous Cornish Pasties. I hadn't realized he was familiar with Conner's specialty, since he rarely left Darklane. Apparently his powers extended farther than I thought, and he knew where to get the best grub in town.

When we pulled up to Aethelred's door in Darklane, the part of town where the dark magic practitioners hung out, it didn't look like anyone was home. The curtains were drawn on the narrow windows of the tall row home. Like all the rest, the home's exterior was a soot-covered Victorian building with intricate architecture and bright paint peeking out from beneath the grime. In Aethelred's case, the house was blue. Or it had been once.

I climbed out of Aidan's car, the bag of pasties clutched in my fist. I'd snuck one on the way here—a beef and potato that had been delightful—so I was no longer hungry. Hopefully Aethelred wouldn't notice that the bag wasn't *quite* full.

"It's always so dark here," I said. It was like the tall, narrow buildings blocked out the sun. Or the taint of dark magic polluted the place.

"It's not my favorite part of town, either," Aidan said as he climbed the narrow steps ahead of me and rapped on the door, using the brass falcon door knocker.

The door opened immediately, and a wizened old man dressed in a navy velour track suit peered out at us from behind silver spectacles. His beard reached all the way to his waist, part of it tucked into his trousers. Like before, I couldn't help but think of him as Gandalf in athleisure wear.

"Hi, Aethelred." I held out the bag.

He snatched it and peered inside. "Good. Though I see you ate one."

"Nuh uh. It's full." Had he used his seer ability to spy on me?

"You have pastry on your lip."

I rubbed at my lip, and a piece of flaky pastry crust fluttered to the ground. I glanced at Aidan for backup, but he just shook his head, unwilling to lie to an old man for me. Damned honorable Shifter.

"I was poison checking," I said.

"Sure. Because Connor dopes up his pasties."

"Fair point. He doesn't. Could we come in?"

"Oh, all right." He stepped back and gestured us into his dark little foyer.

We followed him into a dimly lit living room. Shelves lined every wall, stuffed full of books and trinkets. Dust motes glittered in the light that streamed through pulled shades. I caught sight of the *Magic's Bend Times* lying on the coffee table. It said today was a Tuesday. Things had been so crazy, it'd been hard to keep track. Tuesday was Black Bingo night, if I recalled correctly.

"Going to Black Bingo tonight?" I asked, hoping that a little conversation about his interests would endear us to him. Aethelred loved Black Bingo. According to our mutual friends Aerdeca and Mordaca, he hadn't missed a game in a decade.

"Yes," he grumbled. "That's what the pasties are for. It's my turn to cater."

"Hmmm. Glad we could help."

"Well, it wasn't done out of the goodness of your heart. Why are you here?"

I winced, though he was right. I really should work on the goodness of my heart.

"We need some help. I was hoping you could scry for us."

His gaze traveled to Aidan. "For the right price, maybe. Though you still owe me some transportation charms."

"I know." We'd borrowed some from him last month. "But there's been a shortage. We don't have a single one ourselves."

Which put us at a huge disadvantage to Victor.

"We think the shortage is the fault of the man we want you to scry for," Aidan said.

"Is this the same man who tried to destroy the Museum of Magical History? Who threatened my home?"

"The very same," Aidan said. "So you can understand why this is important. And we'll replace the transportation charms. On my honor."

"And you'll pay my fee for scrying," Aethelred said.

Aidan inclined his head. "Of course."

"A very hefty fee." Aethelred's blue eyes gleamed. "I have my eye on a beach cottage."

"Of course," Aidan said.

"Good." Aethelred set the paper bag of pasties on the table and sat on the ratty armchair, then gestured for us to sit on the equally ratty couch. "What do you want to know?"

"Three things," I said as I sat. "Victor Orriodor is apparently seeking a greater power as part of his plan to destroy the Alpha Council. What does that mean? And what kind of protections does his home in Transylvania have? Are there prisoners inside?" I didn't say what kind of prisoners, as even Aethelred didn't know I was a FireSoul. My concealment charm wouldn't let him see that information about me.

"Your villain lives in Transylvania?" Aethelred chuckled. "Of course he does. Well, I can look for these things, but I make no promises about what I will be able to see."

"Thank you," I said.

Aethelred sat back in his chair and closed his eyes. It was all I could do not to bounce my knee impatiently.

Seers couldn't see everything, but what they could see was true.

After a period of time that felt like a century—I checked Aidan to see if his dark hair had turned white—Aethelred sat forward and opened his eyes.

"I cannot see much about his plans for the Alpha Council or the greater power that you mention," he said. "That's quite oblique, you know."

"Yeah, I know. It's the best I've got, though."

"All I can say is that I get a dark feeling about it. Whatever he is seeking is dangerous. I believe he wants to use you and your two friends Phoenix and Delphine to get it. That is all I could see."

I knew that already, though I nodded gratefully.

"But I could see his home in Transylvania. I believe it is his primary residence now. And I think it's something you'd like to see as well."

"How can we see it?"

Aethelred got up and shuffled toward a large mirror tucked into a corner. The ornate gold frame was covered in a thick layer of dust, but the glass was clean. I followed him to the mirror, Aidan at my back.

Aethelred reached out a gnarled hand and touched the glass. When he closed his eyes, a smoky image appeared in the mirror. The gray haze coalesced to form shapes. Soon, a massive fortress was visible, perched on craggy black mountains. A dim moon peeked out from behind hazy clouds.

"Whoa," I breathed.

It was the scariest, most intensely fortified place I'd ever seen. My skin prickled as I looked at it, as if the castle's protection charms were so strong they reached through the glass. Slowly, the image zoomed in, as if Aethelred were concentrating on specific parts. Figures began to appear, demons standing on the ramparts, armed with swords and bows.

"Holy shit, there's a lot of them," Aidan said.

"Exactly." Aethelred removed his hand and stepped back. "I couldn't count the number of guards, there were so many. There are also prisoners in the dungeon, though there are protections on the fortress that prohibited me from seeing inside."

"That's a problem," I said.

"That whole place is a problem," Aethelred said. "I could feel the evil in it. Normally, my visions only allow me sight. But this was stronger. Worse. You need to stop that man. Whatever he wants, it is very, very bad."

We said goodbye to Aethelred, but didn't speak to each other until we reached the car. Once I'd climbed in and shut the door, I turned to Aidan.

He spoke first. "The only way to stop Victor is to bring the fight to him. If we wait until he attacks, he'll have the upper hand."

"We could try going to the League of FireSouls for help. Rescuing FireSouls is what they do." I'd met the League just last week. They were a secret organization dedicated to protecting our kind. My parents had been part of their number. "But there really aren't enough of them. Only nine."

Aidan nodded sharply. "That's not enough. We need the Alpha Council. They have far greater numbers than the League."

"You're right. And this is the Alpha Council's fight. Victor is after *them*. They're the ones who killed his innocent parents and turned him into a monster." I winced. That sounded a lot like victim blaming. "That's not to say they deserve to have him after their blood, but they should help with this. They've handled FireSouls poorly in the past, and this is the result."

"They can help us break through the guards," Aidan said. "Let them fight Victor, who is after their blood, while we go rescue the FireSouls in his dungeon. We can get them out of there while the Alpha Council is busy with Victor."

"It's a good plan."

Aidan wearily scrubbed a hand over his face. "But it's risky. I don't want you near the Alpha Council unless you have to be."

"So we'll go warn them about what Dermot is up to and request their help."

"There's no *we*," Aidan said. "I'm still going alone to request their help."

I bristled, wanting to be involved with every step. But he was right. I could blow this for us if they figured out what I was.

"Okay." I nodded. "But you'll wear a comms charm so that I can hear what's going on. And I'll be nearby in case you need help."

"Fine. Good solution. This will work."

"I hope so."

# CHAPTER FIVE

The sun was setting as we pulled up to the Fairfield Airport, which was located on the outskirts of Magic's Bend. The airport was tiny, and having Aidan's private jet made things even easier. We'd fly into a small airport run by supernaturals over in Scotland, thereby avoiding customs and lines on the other side of the journey as well.

Nix and Del were waiting on the tarmac when Aidan and I pulled up. I'd called to tell them our plan and to ask them to bring my bag. They'd left Emile with Connor and Claire.

Aidan stopped the car near the jet.

"I'll see you on the plane," Aidan said. "I need to go check with the pilot about takeoff."

"Sure."

Aidan and I climbed out of the big SUV. He handed his keys to his assistant, who'd also met us, then set off for the plane. I headed over to Del and Nix.

"Get some good info?" Del asked as I approached. She had a bag slung over her shoulder, and her black hair spilled over the pink, U-shaped airplane pillow slung around her neck.

"Yeah, before it all went to shit."

She frowned. "What do you mean?"

"I lost control of my power and dropped a house on Dermot and his guards," I said. "They're all dead."

The words made bile threaten to rise in my throat. Aidan's men had called us when they'd arrived a few minutes ago, letting us know they'd found an Order of the Magica cleanup crew at Dermot's house. They'd asked some questions and learned that everyone in the rubble was dead. But at least they didn't know who'd destroyed the house.

"Damn." Nix grimaced.

"Yeah. I'll update you with what we learned on the plane."

"Sounds good." She handed me my overnight bag. "Here's your stuff."

"Thanks." I took the duffle from her.

"So we're off to the Alpha Council headquarters?" Del asked.

"Aidan is. I'm backup in case he needs help." I glanced at Del's airplane pillow, knowing where this was going. "No need for you to risk being around them."

The Alpha Council had proven how gung-ho they were about capturing FireSouls. I'd first seen Emile a couple months ago when they were dragging him off to the Prison for Magical Miscreants. I didn't want my *deirfiúr* anywhere near them.

"Ha," Nix said. "You can forget that right now. We're going with you. Even if we don't go inside."

"Yeah," Del said. "Letting you handle this on your own is no longer okay with us. We're a team, remember?"

I grinned. There was no point fighting them, and they could handle themselves. "All right."

Nix held up another bag. "Anyway, I've already packed my best kilt."

"And I've got my pillow." Del poked the pink fluff around her neck.

"Who can argue with that?" I said.

"Then off to Scotland!" Del cried.

The plane took off without incident, for which I was grateful. There'd been so many shocks and ambushes lately that I was wired for them.

After a dinner of lasagna and wine that the plane's catering company had provided, we discussed Victor Orriodor and what Aidan and I had learned from Dermot and Aethelred. Nix and Del agreed that we'd need the Alpha Council's help if we wanted to attack Victor on his home turf. There were just too many guards to do it alone.

Our priorities would be freeing the FireSoul prisoners and destroying Victor.

Until now, I'd been so busy trying to survive that the possibility of other captured FireSouls had been distant.

Now I had confirmation. And a massive amount of power I could use to free them.

"Right, I'm headed to bed." I rose. "You guys good out here?"

Del glanced around the private jet like I was crazy. There were two big couches near the back, each draped with cozy throws.

"I'll persevere." Del petted the pink airline pillow around her neck. "And I don't think I'm going to need this fellow."

I left Del and Nix to stretch out on the couches in the main cabin and headed to the small bedroom at the back of the plane. There were perks to dating the owner. Though honestly, I'd have been with Aidan even if he were a pizza delivery guy.

I slipped into the dimly lit room. Aidan had preceded me and was already standing by the bed in his tight boxer briefs.

The fabric clung to him indecently, and it was hard to keep my gaze on his face. Apparently shameless was my middle name.

"Are you objectifying me?" There was a smile in Aidan's voice.

I jerked my gaze up from where it'd been glued to his rigid abdomen and grinned.

"You can hardly blame me." I gestured up and down his body. "You're standing there all…"

He grinned, then climbed into the bed. I stripped down to my t-shirt and panties and climbed in next to him. He tugged me against him and held me, my back pressed to his wide chest. I flicked off the bedside lamp and leaned back. In the sudden dark, all the problems we faced loomed larger.

"We'll save them, right?" I asked.

"Yes." His voice sounded so sure that it comforted me. "And we'll reunite them with their families."

"Good." I relaxed against him.

His warm lips had dipped to my neck, tracing along the sensitive skin. I shivered.

"And then we'll go away on a trip," Aidan said. "Just you and me."

"Oh yeah?" I asked.

"Yeah." He nipped my neck, his teeth sending a shudder of pleasure through me. I rolled over to face him and looked into his eyes. It was nearly dark in the room, but there was enough light that I could see the glint of gray.

"So, this is all very stressful," I murmured.

"It is." His voice was rough.

"But I can think of a way to relieve some of that stress." I pressed a kiss to his strong jaw. "But you'll have to promise to be quiet."

He groaned low in his throat, an animal noise that vibrated against my chest.

"You promise?" I asked. "No sound. Your plane doesn't have the best soundproofing."

His strong hand gripped my waist and tugged me to him. He was warm and hard against me, his big body dwarfing mine. Aidan might be bigger than me, but I was the one in control right now.

He dipped his head to mine and feathered his lips across my own. "I promise. But I'm not sure you're going to manage it."

I grinned. "I'll do my best."

A change in the plane's engine noise woke me. Aidan was no longer in the room, but I could still feel his presence. He must have just left.

I scrubbed my eyes and leaned over to peer out the little window. It looked like we were landing. On this side of the Atlantic, the sun was shining, highlighting the peaks and valleys of the Highlands. The airport was supposed to be just outside of Inverness in northeastern Scotland.

I climbed out of bed, thoughts of Aidan filling my mind. There was no question that I was falling hard and fast for him. The big L-word loomed at the edges of my mind, but it freaked me out enough that I shoved it aside easily. I'd never felt that for anyone but my *deirfiúr*. And it was a different sort of L-word with Aidan. I'd save that until we didn't have so much to overcome.

I pulled on my clothes, then grabbed my bag and joined Aidan and my *deirfiúr* in the main cabin. The smell of coffee made my mouth water, and I gratefully accepted a cup from Nix.

"We're landing in fifteen minutes," Aidan said. "Better take a seat."

I strapped in to one of the normal plane seats and sipped my coffee, mentally prepping myself for the meeting with the Alpha Council tomorrow morning.

When we landed, our plane was the only one on the tarmac. Cool wind whipped my hair back from my face as I climbed down the stairs. The mountains that rose on either side of us were green with summer foliage, though there were few trees.

"There's our ride." Aidan pointed to a Range Rover with big wheels parked nearby. A young man leaned against the hood, tossing the keys into the air and catching them again.

"Thank you, Alex," Aidan said as he took the keys from the man. "Give my best to your mum."

"Will do, sir." Alex grinned and headed off toward the only building on the tarmac.

We all climbed into Aidan's car and set off toward his remote childhood home. It was so deep in the boonies that sheep were the only witnesses to our progress, their beady eyes trained on our car.

When we reached Aidan's land, the car rolled slowly through the familiar protective spells that prickled against my skin. Aidan's dad, a fugitive from the Alpha Council fifteen years ago, had decked this place out in protective charms before he'd died. My concealment charm had started working again, keeping me hidden from Victor Orriodor's seers, but the added protection on Aidan's property made me feel even more secure.

"Home sweet home," Aidan said as he pulled up to the shack where he'd lived for part of his youth. His tone indicated that this was in no way a *sweet home*. Even his shoulders were tense. I knew he didn't like this place, and his tension reminded me how much.

But it was perfectly located in relation to Glencarrough, the Alpha Council headquarters, and it was well protected.

"Thanks for letting us use this place," I said as I climbed out of the car.

"Not a problem," Aidan said.

I didn't think he realized that he was scowling at the wooden front door. It was a problem for Aidan to be here—he'd spent some miserable childhood years here—but he pushed that aside for me, and I appreciated it.

I reached out and squeezed his hand. He looked down at me, a small smile tugging at the side of his mouth.

"You know me pretty well, don't you?" he murmured.

"Getting there," I said.

He pressed a kiss to my forehead, then set off toward the house. The sun was heading toward the horizon as Nix, Del, and I followed him. The earlier warmth had departed, leaving a bite to the air despite the fact that it was late summer.

Aidan stepped onto the stoop and ran his hands along the perimeter of the wooden door, unlocking the protection spell. When the spell deactivated, some of the prickling feeling of the charm dissipated. My shoulders loosened.

Aidan pushed on the door and stepped inside, waving his hand to ignite the lanterns scattered around the cottage. They burst to life with a golden glow, illuminating the rustic kitchen that held only an ancient refrigerator, sink, and some dinged-up counters. The living room and dining nook were tiny, the furnishings rough.

"I'm going to drop my stuff in the bedroom, then head out to practice my magic," I said.

"I'll come," Aidan said.

"I don't think that's a good idea." I thought of the roof I'd dropped on Dermot and the sonic boom that I'd knocked my friends out with before. "I don't want to pulverize your insides if I get it wrong."

"Yeah, she's pretty dangerous." Del rubbed her chest, no doubt in memory of the blast I'd hit her with last week when my new magic had gone awry. "You should listen to her."

"All right," Aidan said. "I'll cut some wood for the fire. You have an hour. After that, I'm coming for you."

"Deal." He could test how I was controlling my signature. I was definitely much better at keeping my secret when I used my magic, but my new power made it more difficult. I thought I had a handle on it, but I sure wouldn't mind confirming that.

I dropped my bag in the bedroom I'd used before, then headed out to the kitchen.

"Good luck," Nix said. "Call us on your comms charm if you need us."

"Will do." I zipped up my jacket as I stepped out into the cool air.

The woods were silent as I made my way through the forest to the clearing on the east side of Aidan's land. I'd practiced my powers there once before, learning to shift into a fox. It felt like ages ago, though it hadn't even been two months.

I cleared my mind as I walked, calling upon my power to enhance my hearing, a talent that I'd gained by stealing a Shifter's gift. The forest was no longer silent. Leaves rustled and squirrels chittered. I'd be able to hear anyone sneak up on me.

My stolen Shifter senses were such an asset.

I shoved my hands into my pockets and hunched my shoulders. Prickly guilt streaked through me at the thought of Lorena, the wolf Shifter whose power I'd stolen. She'd been a bad person—she'd enslaved a child named Amara and tried to give her to Victor. I didn't doubt that she'd done terrible things and deserved to be punished.

But had I needed to be the one to mete out that punishment? Should it have been death? When I'd killed her and taken her power, I'd thought she deserved it.

But I hadn't been thinking about how she'd been acting out of grief, seeking vengeance for the death of her father. What would I do if someone killed Nix or Del?

I wouldn't hurt a child, but I'd probably go on some kind of rampage. Her grief didn't justify her actions. But her actions didn't justify mine, either.

I wished I hadn't killed her.

My thoughts ricocheted inside my head as I thought about everything I'd done and had yet to do. Over the last two months, so much had changed. I'd embraced my magic. I'd gained many new skills, often by killing and taking them. I could throw lightning, shift into a wolf, use the power of illusion to confuse my enemies.

I'd taken these powers to help protect myself and my *deirfiúr*. And I'd only taken them from people who had offered or who were trying to kill me.

I hadn't been an outright evil murderer or anything, but I hadn't been entirely good, either.

But from here on out, I wouldn't take any more. I was strong enough. I had enough power. I just needed to learn to wield it.

I reached the clearing and stopped, running my fingertips over the golden dampening cuff I wore. This cuff made me almost normal, repressing my new magic to the point that I had access to only part of it.

But I needed it all if I was going to win.

I removed the cuff. Soul-shaking power flowed through me, lighting me up like a live wire. I trembled with power, magic coursing through me like a drug, and I let my breath whoosh out of me. Once I was steady, I set the cuff on a fallen log nearby and then straightened.

I took stock of the magic flowing through my veins. This was some serious stuff. But massive power wasn't any good if it went out of control and hurt those I loved.

So I needed practice.

I would start with illusion. If that went awry, it hopefully wouldn't start a forest fire or something. It seemed too dangerous to start with my lightning. I wasn't yet ready to see the size of the bolt I could create with this amount of juice. Probably something comparable to an atom bomb. And I didn't really want to be in the atom bomb business.

I tried to relax as I focused on the magic within me. It sparked and fizzed, almost a living thing, eager to be let out of its cage. I called on it, pushing it outward toward the trees as I envisioned an old-fashioned party that I'd seen in a movie with Del and Nix a few months ago. It was more a ball than a party, and I did my best to pretend I was back in time.

Colors flashed before my eyes. Enormous dresses on the women and men in strange suits, all lit by glittering chandeliers. I imagined the music as the dancers began to form around me, their colorful forms flitting between the trees.

Magic still vibrated under my skin, raging to be let out. I released some more, envisioning the band that had been in the corner of the massive ballroom. Slowly, they formed. Then the walls of the place appeared, covered in yellow silk wallpaper. The ceiling was supported by thick white columns.

Soon, I stood inside of history, the dancers swirling around me. My heart swelled even as my magic began to surge within me, pushing to break free. Joy at my accomplishment was overwhelmed by panic.

I was losing control of the magic. My skin sparked, little pricks of light flying off of me as the magic seeped out of my pores.

Is this what had happened when I'd lost control before and knocked out all my friends? The magic had exploded out of me and hurt them?

Only it was happening more slowly now, little rays of light shining from me.

Which meant I could control it.

I *had* to control it.

I tried to rein the magic back in, calming my breathing and my mind. But I didn't let go of the illusion. Quitting wasn't practice. I had to keep the illusion going while I controlled my magic.

But the dancers blurred in front of my eyes, turning transparent in places. The forest peaked through the illusion, trees bisecting bodies and walls.

My lungs felt tight and the air thick as soup. Hot, too. The light shined more brightly from me, cutting through the dancers like sunlight through a vampire.

I clenched my fists, reaching to hold on to the magic. To keep the illusion going. But pain sliced through my mind, so sharp and bright that I stumbled to my knees.

*Shit.*

"Cass!" Aidan's voice cut through the forest.

Magic exploded out from me, a concussive force that blasted through the trees. It tore off tree limbs and blew dirt into the air.

Through bleary eyes, I saw Aidan on his knees about ten yards away.

*Damn it.*

Groggily, I climbed to my feet and raked my sweaty hair back from my face, then staggered over to Aidan. He was getting to his feet, his face wan.

"Are you all right?" I asked.

"Fine." His color was returning. "You're gaining control."

"Gaining it? I totally lost it at the end there."

"Maybe, but not nearly as bad as last time."

I wasn't sure if he meant the time I'd dropped a house on Dermot or knocked Aidan unconscious, but either way... "You have a point."

"I usually do. And on the plus side, I can't really sense your magic right now."

Hope fluttered in my chest. "That's a good thing, at least."

Aidan pressed a kiss to my forehead. "It's definitely a good thing. You're gaining control. But come on. We'll have dinner. Then you can practice more if you want."

My stomach grumbled at the mention of dinner. "Good plan."

And I would practice more. Because what I was working with now wasn't enough to keep my friends safe or to defeat Victor. Not by a long shot.

# CHAPTER SIX

At ten 'til ten the next morning, Aidan's car crested the hill in front of Glencarrough. Nix and Del had stayed behind, but they had Del's comms charms in case I needed to call for backup. Del had saved up her power, so she was ready to transport to us in an instant. Aidan was wearing Nix's charm so that I could listen in.

Aidan pulled over on the side of the road, hiding the car mostly behind a patch of scrubby trees. I looked down at his destination, an enormous stone structure crouched between two hulking mountains. The Alpha Council headquarters was a monstrosity of towers and walls that spread across a Highland valley in central Scotland.

"This place gives me the creeps," I said. When I'd first seen this place, I'd thought it looked like a fairytale villain's castle. It wasn't as bad as Victor's definitely haunted castle, but it was plenty scary.

"Me too," Aidan said. Sheep scurried in front of the car, their little white legs kicking up as they bounded away. "I didn't like growing up at my father's hovel, but this place was no better."

Though I remembered the inside of Glencarrough as being beautiful, the outside did not reflect that. And it was full of Shifters who hated FireSouls. I sure hoped Aidan didn't need my help in there.

Aidan pulled out some binoculars and peered through them at the walls, then handed them to me. I raised them, having to move them around a bit to find a patch through the scrubby trees.

At least two dozen guards paced the ramparts. Quickly, I dropped the binoculars. They couldn't see us well through our cover, but we needed to be quick.

"I don't think they've replaced the Heartstone yet," I said.

"Yeah." Aidan peered up at the guards. "There'd be far fewer guards if they had."

"So you know what you're heading into," I said.

"I do." He leaned over and kissed me quickly, then said, "You should shift now."

I nodded, reaching out for his magic, getting ready to mirror his ability to turn into any animal. Though I could turn into a wolf with my own stolen power, I needed to be a bird for this.

Aidan would drive through the gates alone. I would stay outside, shifted into falcon form. If he needed my help, I could fly over the ramparts and rescue him. Hopefully no one would think twice of one native bird. Once inside, I could use my powers—illusion, lightning, whatever it took—to get him out of whatever pickle he was in.

"I really don't think you need to do this, though," Aidan said. "It will be fine."

"I know it will. I just want to be on hand in case it isn't, okay?"

He nodded sharply.

I grinned, taking off my comms charm and handing it to him, then let the magic flow through me, warming my limbs. A second later, the world flashed before my eyes, and I shrunk into falcon form.

I sat on the passenger seat as Aidan shortened the cord on my comms charm and fastened it around my neck. It hung a bit awkwardly, but it worked. I'd have preferred to shift into a sparrow or smaller bird, but they weren't big enough to support the weight of the charm.

He touched his charm and said, "I'll be back soon."

The words echoed out of the charm around my neck, and I tilted my head as a nod. The charms worked.

Aidan lowered the car's side window, and I hopped onto the window sill and flew out, catching the breeze beneath my wings.

I flew away from Aidan's car, approaching Glencarrough from the south. About a quarter mile from the gates, I found a tree branch to sit on so that I could watch.

Aidan's car pulled up to the gate and stopped.

"See you when this is over," he said through the comms charm.

A heavy groaning noise came from the charm, the heavy wooden gate lifting.

This was it.

My feathers prickled.

I watched him drive through, catching sight of a man with wild yellow hair walking along the ramparts, then disappearing, presumably down some stairs.

Only one man had hair like that. Mathias. The lion Shifter who knew I was a FireSoul, but who'd kept my secret. I'd managed to convince him I wasn't a threat, but it'd been hard. I doubted I could convince the rest of the Council if they figured out what I was. I may have helped them save Amara, the little girl who'd tended the Heartstone, but that wouldn't buy me complete immunity from their fears and superstitions.

"Mathias is approaching," Aidan murmured through the charm.

I could just imagine Mathias walking down the long steps pressed against the interior wall of Glencarrough. He'd greeted me from that direction last time I visited.

I heard a car door slam and assumed that Aidan had gotten out of the car and stepped into the enormous cobblestone courtyard of Glencarrough. As I remembered it, cars would be parked at the edges in front of the large stone buildings.

Worry gnawed at me. There were at least a hundred Shifters in there, many of whom would be watching Aidan from their position guarding the walls. Aidan was more powerful than any of them, but he was vastly outnumbered.

"You're back soon," Mathias's voice echoed through my comms charm.

"I have something important to discuss," Aidan said.

"It's a good thing that Cass didn't come," Mathias said in a low voice. "I worry about the others sensing her signature."

"They haven't been suspicious otherwise?" Aidan asked.

"No. I've heard nothing. She's best off keeping a low profile."

"I'll see that she does," Aidan said.

I bristled, but knew he meant the best.

"The Council is waiting for you," Mathias said.

"Lead the way," Aidan said.

There was silence for a while, and I pictured them walking through the grand entranceway into the main building. Marble floors and silk wallpaper adorned the large foyer, as I recalled. Rare weapons lined the walls. I'd wanted to pocket one last time I'd been there, but I didn't steal. No matter how much my dragon side wanted me to. I was a treasure hunter, but I followed careful rules.

They were probably in the hallway by now. It was there that I'd seen the Alpha Council guards dragging Emile to their dungeon.

I assumed they were going to the Council room—a massive, ornate affair that screamed wealth and power. The Alphas of all the clans would be there.

The sound of light, running footsteps echoed through the comms charm. I focused hard, trying to hear.

"Aidan!" a young voice called.

I recognized that voice. It was Amara, the little girl we'd rescued from Victor. I pictured her in my mind, a slender, dark-haired girl of about nine. She always had a ragged stuffed bunny clutched in her arms.

"Amara!" Aidan's voice echoed through the charm. He sounded happy to see her. I imagined him kneeling and hugging her. "How are you?" Aidan asked.

"Good! We're making a new Heartstone!" she said.

A gruff voice said, "That's enough, Amara."

That would be Amara's father, Angus. I was sure of it. He hadn't liked me when he'd met me before. Thought I smelled funny. Good thing I wasn't in there, as much as I might like to see Amara for myself.

"We're late for our meeting, Angus," Mathias said. "Excuse us."

There was silence for a moment, and then Mathias said, "Aidan Merrick to see you, Alphas."

So they were in the Council room now. I imagined all the Alphas turning to look at Aidan from their seats at the round table. I waited for their greeting, but there was only silence.

Shouldn't they be saying something? Fear chilled my blood.

Suddenly, an angry voice broke through the silence.

"That is the one I told you about. The accomplice to the FireSoul, Cass Clereaux."

"Dermot Mulvey," Aidan's voice was cold. "Aren't you looking well."

Dermot was alive? How? Shock rooted me to the tree.

"Is it true, Aidan?" a feminine voice asked. Elenora, the leader, if I had to guess.

"He doesn't know what he is talking about," Aidan said. "Dermot Mulvey is—"

His words cut off, and a loud crash sounded.

I cried out in surprise. What was happening?

"Dermot! You didn't have to knock him out!" Elenora yelled.

"Lock him in the dungeon," Dermot said. "You can't trust him. When he comes to, you can speak to him there."

"I agree with Dermot," a masculine voice said.

Other people agreed.

I heard a rustling noise. They were dragging him off.

My heart pounded as I pushed off the tree limb, taking to the sky. I flew as fast as I could toward the tower wall. I needed to reach Aidan.

What would I do once I was in?

Figure it out. Use invisibility. Steal a key to the dungeon. Something.

The wind cut through my feathers as I neared the walls. I'd approach from the back, where there were fewer guards. I was just a bird, so they were unlikely to notice me, but better safe than sorry.

I swooped low over the rampart walls, staying far from the men who paced, their eyes ever alert.

I was about to land when I heard a shout.

"Intruder!"

*No!*

I was just a bird! How had they sensed me? I didn't have time to panic. Something heavy crashed over me, dragging me to the ground. I shifted as I fell, my transformation forced by the magic in the net.

When I slammed to the ground, pain radiated through my body. I lay there on the cobblestone courtyard, stunned, able to feel all the magic in the air. Beneath my cheek was a strange, star-shaped ornament inset into the cobblestones. I stared at it dazedly as I tried to get my bearings.

The signatures of the many Shifters bombarded me—tastes, smells, sounds. So many Shifters in one area gave the place a buzzing feeling.

I scrambled upright, throwing the net off me. Before I could call upon my magic, something sharp pierced me in the neck. I reached up, feeling a dart of some kind.

Then I passed out.

Cold crept along my skin, seeping deep within my bones and dragging me from slumber. The bed beneath me was hard as rock. I curled my hand against it, realizing that it *was* rock. Hard and gritty stone.

My head pounded as I opened my eyes. Four stone walls surrounded me. A heavy wooden ceiling stretched above. I turned my head to see a wooden door, reinforced with iron strips. There was nothing in the room except me.

My power was suppressed. Not even a spark of it burned within me. I pulled off the golden dampener cuff at my wrist, but my magic stayed repressed. There were some seriously powerful anti-magic charms on this cell. Shifters couldn't do magic like Magica could, so of course their prison would have strong enchantments against it.

*I was in another freaking prison.*

Helpless rage made me clench my fists as I jerked upright. My brain throbbed, feeling like it bounced against my skull.

Aidan was gone. Possibly in his own cell.

And I was locked up.

Again.

But Dermot was alive. Aidan's men had reported that the Order said all the bodies in the rubble were dead. Dermot must have survived without injury and escaped before the Order showed up.

The bastard must have used one of his protective shields to save himself from the falling roof. The only person I'd wanted to kill had been the one to survive.

He must have realized we'd come here to rat him out, so he'd beaten us to it. Barely. But it'd been enough time to sow the seeds of doubt in the minds of the Alpha Council members.

I almost growled, but the noise was cut off by the sound of a key in the lock. I jumped to my feet and raced to the door, tucking myself beside it so that whoever was entering couldn't see me.

They'd taken the daggers I'd had strapped to my thighs, but I was still a good fighter. And I had my other charms. I just had to get away from the dampening charm that had been put on this cell. Then I could really fight my way free.

The door creaked open and I tensed, ready to pounce. A massive grizzly bear stalked into the room, his claws as big as steak knives. He smelled like salmon and old dirt, and his fangs were longer than my forearm.

I sank back against the wall.

A woman in a long green dress followed the bear into the cell. Her brown hair was pulled back and streaked liberally with gray. Elenora. The wolf Shifter who was the leader of the Alpha Council. We'd been on friendly terms when I'd helped save Amara. I hadn't expected her to be my buddy, but tossing me in this barren cell was a bit much.

"Why am I here?" I demanded.

She turned her sharp gaze on me. The bear at her side growled.

"Shut up, Smokey," I said.

Her brows rose. "I'd think you'd be on your best behavior, considering your circumstances."

I glanced around. "Oh, this? I'm used to it." I made my voice sharp. "But I shouldn't be in here. Not after how I proved myself with Amara. I saved your niece's life. At great risk to my own, might I remind you. You said that I went above and beyond. Those were your exact words."

"I recall. But you broke into Glencarrough. Did you think we wouldn't notice an unidentified bird? We're very sensitive to other animals. They don't come here. Only Shifters do. And Dermot Mulvey, a high-ranking member of the Order of the Magica, has leveled some serious accusations against you."

"That I'm a FireSoul? Ridiculous."

"Of course you're a FireSoul. While you were passed out, we had our healer check your magical signature. You are most definitely a FireSoul." Her green eyes took on a thoughtful sheen. "I always thought your magic smelled odd."

"The Origin wouldn't spend time with a FireSoul," I said. "No way."

"Aidan Merrick will do whatever suits him," she said. "As you well know."

She was right about that.

"Give up the charade." Elenora crossed her arms elegantly in front of her chest.

She was right. I was found out. "Aidan doesn't know what I am."

"Lie," she said.

"He doesn't." I'd go to my grave maintaining that.

"I appreciate that you are trying to protect him."

I scowled at her. "Where is Aidan?"

"He's in the cell down the hall. You're here in this cell because you're a FireSoul, and we don't know what to do with you."

I wanted to growl at her. Had she so quickly forgotten the risks I'd taken for Amara? But Dermot must have pleaded his case well.

"Don't know?" I scoffed. "Toss me in the Prison for Magical Miscreants, obviously." I'd escape on the way there, hopefully.

"Normally, yes. But as you said, you helped us with Amara. At great risk to yourself. I believe that you are fundamentally good, Cassiopeia. Your species has a well-deserved reputation for evil—how could you not, given the amount of power you can wield? But I believe you are the exception to that rule."

Little did she know, I had more power than she could dream of. "You're wrong. I'm not an exception. Most FireSouls are harmless."

"Oh?" Her brows rose. "You've met others?"

I cursed myself inwardly. Now was not the time to be defending my species. I had to play it smart and safe and selfish and get my ass out of here. "I knew some when I was a child. But you believe I'm an exception—that I'm fundamentally good—so you're locking me up here?"

"It's better than turning you in to the prison or the Order of the Magica. The Shifters know what you've done for us. So we're going to take some time and figure out what is going on. If we can trust you not to harm us, we will release you."

"What did Dermot tell you is going on?"

"That you are a FireSoul who robbed him. And that you are involved in a plot to take down the Alpha Council and Glencarrough."

That sneaky bastard. How smart of him to tell her I was doing exactly what he planned. Now what was I supposed to say? *Nuh uh, that's* his *plan?*

"Why would I want to take down the Alpha Council?" It was all I could say.

"A vendetta against those who imprison your kind."

I laughed. "Really? That's the dumbest thing I've ever heard. If I had a vendetta against people who were assholes to FireSouls, it'd be everybody!"

"That was my thought. Unless the Alpha Council hurt you specifically, I can't imagine why you'd start by targeting us."

"Exactly. So you can let me out."

The grizzly growled at that, stepping forward. I hissed at him.

"No, I cannot," Elenora said. "While I might be willing to, other members of the Council are not. They want more answers."

"Fine. You can have them." I told her about Dermot and Victor Orriodor. Her brows rose as the story continued. When I finished, she looked skeptical rather than worried.

For the first time, my heart really sank.

"That's an interesting story," she said. "You can understand why I am wary of it, however. Dermot is part of the Order of the Magica. Why would he want our downfall?"

"I don't know."

"We aren't going to turn you in to the prison or reveal what you are to the Order of the Magica. Not yet. We will keep you here until we confirm your claims."

"You'll need to do it quick, because Victor has plans for you."

"We will do our best. We haven't replaced the Heartstone, so you can understand how this is a matter of utmost importance."

Damn, that was bad. It'd make it so much easier for Victor to break into Glencarrough. As he'd planned.

"I will present what you have said to the Alpha Council," Elenora said. "In the meantime, you will stay here."

I glanced around at the barren cells. "Seriously?"

"We'll bring in some furniture to make it more comfortable. But we can't trust you in the rest of the keep."

I had nothing to say to that.

She turned and walked out.

Right before she left, I asked, "Is Dermot still here?"

"He is not." She left the room, the grizzly at her heels.

I slouched against the wall, my mind racing.

If Dermot and Victor needed me and my *deirfiúr* for the final havoc they planned to wreak, then what good to them was I locked up in here? They couldn't even get to me.

*Shit.*

I almost pounded my head into the wall when I realized. I was such an idiot. If Dermot put us here, it meant he had a way to get us out. Of course. Whatever they planned, it would definitely go down at Glencarrough.

This probably worked out better for them. They couldn't find me and my *deirfiúr* because of our concealment charms. But they could rat us out to the Alpha Council and get us thrown into the dungeons.

Where we'd wait for them to arrive. They'd break in somehow—aided by the fact that the Heartstone was missing and defenses were down—and they'd put their miserable plan into action.

I was one card in their deck, and I'd put myself right into their hands.

# CHAPTER SEVEN

I spent the next hour feeling my way around every stone in the wall and floor, hoping to find an out. Nix and Del would come for me, but I didn't want them to. It'd be the worst thing in the world for them to get caught in this cell, too. Sitting ducks waiting for Victor and Dermot.

And though Del could transport, she probably couldn't do it within the confines of the dungeon because this place would block her magic, too. So it was up to me to find a way out of a stone box.

If only I'd found that last transportation charm when I'd been searching the properties room at the Prison for Magical Miscreants. That'd get me right out of here.

But then, the Alpha Council probably would have taken it from me.

So I'd have been screwed either way.

I stiffened when I heard a shuffle outside the door. Were people coming to deliver furniture, like Elenora had said? I crept over to the side of the door, hoping that maybe this time they wouldn't be bringing a grizzly for a guard.

I stared hard at the door, waiting for it to open. But it didn't. Instead, the black strips of iron that reinforced the wooden door began to glow hot orange. Then they began to drip.

*They were melting.* Long, rolling drips of molten metal slid down the doorframe, pooling on the stone below. My heart pounded in my ears.

A moment later, the door creaked open. As it swung, I noticed that the locking mechanism had melted entirely out of the wood.

Amara peeked her head in. "Cass?"

"Holy shit, Amara." She was busting me out of here.

"I'm half Metal Mage," she said.

"I can see that. I'm so glad to see you."

"Come on. Quick," she said. Her ragged stuffed bunny was clutched in her hand. "No one knows I'm down here."

I went to the door and hopped over the puddle of rapidly cooling metal. As soon as I got into the hall, my magic surged within me, coming back to life.

I hugged her quickly. "Thanks for getting me out of there."

"No problem. You saved me once before. When I heard my dad say you were down here, I had to get you out."

"You'll get in trouble."

She glanced back at the door. "Not like the trouble you were just in. I'll lose screen time and maybe be grounded for a year, but it's worth it."

I grinned. "Thanks."

I didn't like the idea of her being grounded, but the Shifters cherished their kids. Nothing harmful would happen to her besides some solid boredom.

"No problem," Amara said. "Let's get Aidan out."

She led me to a door at the other end of the hall. It was the same construction as mine had been, though there was more metal on the door. Probably because Aidan had more brute strength than me. They weren't taking any chances with the Origin.

"Mind if I borrow your power?" I asked.

"Go ahead."

I touched the widest metal strip that bisected the door and connected to the lock, then reached out for Amara's magic. It felt warm against my skin, and as soon as I had a grip on it, I also felt like I could feel all the metal in the door. Not just the stuff under my fingertips, but all the pieces that were nailed to the other side of the wood as well.

I pushed the magic out of me, concentrating on melting the strips of metal. A second later, the metal liquefied and poured to the ground in a rush.

Amara and I both leapt back to avoid being splashed by the molten iron.

"Wow," Amara said. "You're strong."

"Yeah." I hadn't expected to melt it so quickly. It'd taken Amara almost a minute to melt the metal on my door. I'd done it in a second. "You okay?"

She nodded. "I didn't get burned.'

"Good." I pushed open the door to Aidan's cell, careful not to touch any part of the wood where the iron had been for fear that it might be hot.

As soon as the door swung open, Aidan stepped into the doorway, then jumped over the melted metal and joined us in the hall.

"I thought that might be you," he said. His gaze dropped to Amara. "You came to save us?"

"Yep." She grinned, revealing a missing tooth.

"Good lass." He rubbed her head. "I'll send you a present as a thank you. How does a pony sound?"

"How about a remote control helicopter?" Her eyes gleamed.

"Done."

"Thanks!" Her eyes turned thoughtful. "Address it to my room. I think I'm going to be grounded a while."

"It's a deal," Aidan said. "Now tell us, are there any other exits from Glencarrough?"

"No, just the gate."

"Anything small?" I asked. "A place that rats might sneak in, maybe?"

She screwed up her face as she thought. "There are rats in the kitchens. I like to leave them cheese. I think they come in through the pantry. It's against the main wall, so there might be a way out from there. If you were a rat."

"Good thing I can turn into a rat, then," Aidan said. "Now you run along. Maybe you won't get in trouble for this if you aren't caught."

She looked down at the molten metal. "No one else can do that. So they'll know it was me."

"Thank you extra much, then," Aidan said. "I'll send you two helicopters."

She grinned. "You'd better go."

We hurried down the dungeon hall to the stairs.

I perked my ears, calling upon my heightened senses. When I heard no one coming, I said, "Let's get to the top of the stairs. Then we'll shift into mice. Amara, could you lead us to the kitchen?"

She nodded. "Yeah."

We climbed the stairs silently. At the top, Aidan mouthed, "Now?"

I nodded.

A swirl of silver gray light shimmered around him, then he disappeared. I looked down. At my feet sat a tiny gray mouse. I called on my Mirror Mage powers, reaching out for Aidan's gift. I grasped ahold of it, smelling the forest scent of his magic, and envisioned myself turning into a mouse as well.

Magic warmed me from within, filling up my limbs. Suddenly, I was falling, the walls flashing in front of me. Or I was shrinking rapidly. A moment later, I looked down and saw tiny mouse feet tipped with transparent claws. Next to me, a gray mouse twitched his nose.

Aidan was a bigger mouse than I, but not by much. Amara loomed overhead.

"Ready?" she asked.

I nodded, then scrambled up over the stone stair, digging my claws into the minuscule crevices in the rock. Amara pushed the door open to reveal a wide hallway. It wasn't as ornately decorated as the one we'd walked through before.

Good. That meant we weren't in the main part of the house. Amara headed right, walking quickly down the hall, her ragged bunny slapping against her calf.

Aidan and I raced behind her, keeping ourselves tucked against the wall. Fortunately, the floor was gray stone like the wall, so we blended. If any Shifters came upon us, they'd probably be able to smell us, but hopefully our camouflage would buy us some time.

The world flew by as we ran, looking entirely different from down here. I picked up different scents and sounds and could even feel the thud of Amara's footsteps through my paws. My little mouse lungs were heaving by the time Amara stepped through a doorway into a big, warm kitchen.

A massive man turned to her and grinned. His floppy white mustache made him look like Belle's dad from the cartoon version of *Beauty and the Beast*.

Aidan and I hesitated at the door as Amara walked in.

"And what are you scrounging around for, Miss Amara?" he asked.

Amara walked quickly over to the big fire and sat down, drawing the man's attention away from the door. "Biscuits, Master Murphy. I'm just desperate for some biscuits, and you make the best ones in the world."

I would've laughed if I could have, at how thick she was laying it on.

"Do I now?" Master Murphy asked, his eyes twinkling.

I liked him right away, though I had a feeling he might not take kindly to rodents in his kitchen. I shrank against the wall as I watched.

"Do you have any of the chocolate ones?" Amara asked.

Master Murphy lumbered over to a cupboard. As soon as his back was turned, she pointed toward a narrow door set against the far wall.

The pantry.

I tried to telepathically send her my thanks before racing across the floor, my eyes on the prize. Aidan ran alongside me, his whiskers twitching. I skidded under the door, into the dark pantry. Scents of grain and cheese and dried beans filled my nose.

Heaven. My mouse stomach grumbled, but I ignored it and followed Aidan to the wall on the right. My eyes adjusted to the dim light as we ran along the crevice, searching for a hole.

I smelled it before I saw it, the slightest tinge of fresh air. Near the corner at the back, there was a tiny gap in the stone. Aidan glanced at me with his beady black eyes, then shimmied through the hole.

I followed, scrabbling for purchase to pull myself through. We raced along a tiny corridor made of stone and dirt, going down into the ground before coming back up and out at the exterior wall.

The noon sun was high in the sky by the time we burst free. I blinked blindly, getting my vision back. The exterior wall loomed behind us, feeling a million miles tall in my mouse form. An endless expanse of rolling, heather-clad mountains stretched ahead.

Beside me, a gray light swirled around Aidan's mouse form. A moment later, a small hawk stood in its place, a species that I thought was native to Scotland. It looked like it fit the landscape, at least, with its glinting brown feathers.

I shivered as it looked at me, knowing it was Aidan and that I wasn't really a mouse. But it was still creepy—to be prey eyed by a predator.

I was so anxious to shift that it was easy to reach out and grasp on to Aidan's magic. I envisioned myself as an identical hawk and let the magic flow through me. It filled my limbs with warmth as I grew, my mouse feet shifting to form wings, my snout into a beak.

Aidan's hawk nodded at me, then we pushed off the ground and into the sky. The first few flaps of my wings were a bit awkward, but I let instinct take over. We soared over the mountains, leaving Glencarrough behind.

The wind ruffled my feathers, and joy sang through me. We'd be home in no time.

When the blow hit me from behind, sending me plummeting to the ground, it caught me completely by surprise. Shock scattered my thoughts as I tumbled through the air, my wings flapping helplessly.

Just as I caught the air beneath my wings, a heavy net fell over me, dragging me down. Like before, the magic in the net forced my change back to human. Pain burst through my chest as I hit the ground. Fortunately, heather broke most of my fall.

Aidan crashed to the ground beside me, also trapped in a heavy rope net. My gaze darted around, taking in the sloping mountain ground and the two human figures racing toward us. A lion and a panther ran by their sides.

Shifters. Two transformed, two still human. Above, a massive falcon swooped on the breeze. Another Shifter.

They must have felt us escape and run us down. The men carried big rifles. Whether they were loaded with bullets or darts, it didn't matter. Either could shoot a griffin out of the sky.

We had no transportation charms. There was only one way out of this that didn't involve killing all these Shifters. There was no way the Alpha Council would side with us if we killed them, and I didn't want their blood on my hands.

The men were still a dozen yards away as I darted my hand up to feel for the comms charm that normally hung around my neck, hidden beneath my shirt.

"Del," I said as I glanced at the sun. "We need you to get us out of here! Ten miles west of Glencarrough."

"On it," Del's voice echoed through the charm.

I scrambled out from under the net as Aidan did the same. The men were nearly upon us, one raising his rifle.

Del appeared on the hillside behind the men. She spun in a circle, her gaze finally catching on me. She disappeared, appearing a moment later right next to us. I lunged for her, grabbing her arm.

The men shouted as she reached for Aidan, whose big hand enveloped hers a half second before the ether sucked us away.

We arrived at Aidan's front door, panting. Nix ran out, her eyes wild.

"Thank magic you got them," she said. Worry shined in her green eyes.

"Yeah, thank you." I gasped to get my breath. "That was more exciting than I expected."

"No kidding," Aidan said.

"What happened back there?" Del asked. "I take it that the meeting didn't go so well?"

"Not even close."

Even though the Alpha Council now knew what I was, we'd agreed that the safest place to be was right where we were on Aidan's land. It had been enchanted by his father to withstand an Alpha Council attack, so it was perfect. We didn't need to be here long, anyhow. Just long enough to plan our next move.

First thing I did when I got back was to take a quick shower in the tiny bathroom. When I walked out into the main living area, I was dressed in clean jeans and t-shirt, but sadly without my daggers. I'd be damned if I wouldn't get them back.

In the kitchen, Nix and Del were chatting with Connor and Claire.

For a second, I didn't realize anything was off. Then I did a double take. "Connor? Claire? What are you guys doing here?"

Emile stepped into the house, a load of firewood in his arms, and Ralph and Rufus each sat on one of his shoulders.

"We discussed it and decided you needed help," Claire said.

"You usually do, lately," Connor said.

*Wasn't that the truth.* "Weren't you supposed to go to the League of FireSouls, Emile? So they could help you get your life back together?"

"Eventually." He set the firewood in the small box by the hearth. "But I got to talking with Connor and Claire and heard about what you're up against. And I want to help."

Ralph and Rufus squeaked at me.

"So do they," Emile said with a grin.

"Uh, thanks, guys." I grinned at the rats. They might be small, but they were fierce and clever.

"Your timing is good," Aidan said. "Because we could use the help."

I nodded, though I actually wasn't thrilled to see Connor and Claire. I was happy for their help, but I'd have preferred for them to stay safely out of the way back at P & P. But last time I'd suggested they keep their distance to stay safe, I'd gotten the lecture of a lifetime.

I went to the kitchen and opened the fridge, grateful to see it stocked with a variety of beer, PBR included. That would probably be courtesy of Connor, who usually showed up with a cooler full of goodies. I grabbed a six pack of that and a six pack of Tennent's, a Scottish lager, and went to the table.

"Let's chat," I said.

Connor came to the table, holding a platter stacked with sandwiches.

"You are a hero, Connor." I reached for one and bit in, savoring the hearty turkey and cheese.

Everyone found a seat and reached for a Tennent's, ignoring my beloved PBR.

"So, we've learned some things," I said. I needed to catch Connor, Claire, and Emile up with all the details. Not to mention the new stuff that even Del and Nix were unaware of.

"Give us the deets," Del said.

"So, it goes like this…" I explained everything I'd learned from Dermot, Aethelred, and the Alpha Council. All the puzzle pieces were starting to fall into place, but the puzzle was turning out to be damned scary.

When I finished speaking, Claire leaned back in her chair, her dark eyes serious. "Well, shit. Where is he supposed to get this greater power from? And what form will it take?"

"That's the big question," I said. "I don't know."

"He'll probably use the artifacts he's stolen to perform some kind of spell," Del said.

"But what and where?" Nix asked.

"What, we don't know," Aidan said. "But where is probably on Alpha Council land at Glencarrough."

Emile frowned. "But they refused to listen to you?"

"Yes," I said. "And I don't think we have time to wait. Dermot thinks I'm in the Alpha Council prison. If they really do need me—and maybe Del and Nix—for whatever they've got planned, they're going to want to make their move while they think I'm still locked up."

"So we'll clean up the Alpha Council's mess for them," Claire said. "Fitting."

"I don't see that we have any other choice. I'd bet my life on Victor's end goal resulting in massive casualties."

"And it's going to be soon," Aidan said.

"So what do we do?" Emile asked.

"Attack Victor's creepy castle and cut his legs off. Figuratively speaking," I said.

"Maybe literally, as well." Del smiled menacingly.

"If we can," I said. "But from the vision that Aethelred showed us, Victor's castle is too well protected. This will have to be a stealth mission. Without the Alpha Council, we don't have the numbers. Outright warfare will just get us killed."

"What about asking the League of FireSouls for help."

"They don't have the numbers," I said. "With them, we're up to twenty people. That's not nearly enough. We needed all the Shifters if we had a shot at outright warfare. Victor has more than a hundred demons. With only twenty of us, we don't stand a chance."

"Stealth it is, then," Nix said. "But what's our primary objective?"

"Rescue the FireSouls and steal the artifacts he's been collecting. If we find him unguarded and have the opportunity to kill him, we take it. But our primary focus will be quietly freeing the FireSouls and stealing the artifacts so he doesn't have the tools he needs for his plan."

"What about the Gundestrop cauldron?" Nix asked. "If we take that, it'll dampen our powers. How will we protect ourselves?"

"Maybe we don't take it," I said. "Just the other pieces. He needs everything to make his plan work. And assuming the artifacts are all stored together, we'll only be near the cauldron for a short while."

"And Cass was able to use her magic at the Prison for Magical Miscreants. So she might be able to use it near the cauldron."

"Not much of it, though," I said. "But it's better than nothing. And keep in mind, we're not planning to be seen. So hopefully we won't need our magic to fight." It was a big *hopefully* but it was all we had.

"Afterward, we'll send a message to the Alpha Council," Aidan said. "See if they've changed their minds about believing you. This will buy them a little time to get their act together. Then, once we have their numbers, we fight."

"Good plan," Claire said.

I hoped she was right. Because I was leading my friends straight into the devil's den.

# CHAPTER EIGHT

The wind cut through my feathers as I soared above Victor's Transylvanian castle. We'd flown to Transylvania in Aidan's plane, then gotten a car and driven as far as we could, using Aethelred's directions as a guide.

Somehow, Victor had blocked my FireSoul ability to find him or his artifacts. I'd been able to track them before, so I guessed it had something to do with the protections on his castle.

We'd had to hike the last little bit into the mountains, and now everyone was set up at a makeshift camp about a mile from Victor's castle.

Aidan and I had shifted into small sparrows for this reconnaissance mission, and he flew at my side. Initially, we hadn't known exactly where the castle was located, so we'd gone by air to speed things up. Now that we'd found it, we were searching for the best way into the castle—something sneaky that the guards wouldn't notice.

Unfortunately, it wasn't looking good.

I dipped low on an air current to see how many guards lined the southwest rampart. At least a dozen paced the stone walkway. All demons. Some were clearly shadow demons. The kind who threw smoke bombs. I saw a few red ones. Probably the same type I'd encountered in the pyramid a couple weeks ago. They were armed with flaming swords. The others I didn't recognize, but they would be good fighters. That was a guarantee. My heart pounded, but I pushed away the fear.

We could do this. We *had* to do this.

The castle was almost star-shaped in the way that the walls were built to accommodate the mountain's slopes. But the whole place was massive, with towers and turrets and nooks and crannies. Every inch of it crawling with guards.

It was more suited to an evil mastermind than the mansion at the waypoint where I'd once thought Victor Orriodor lived. It made sense that he'd moved his headquarters.

I veered right on the wind, following Aidan toward the western wall. I saw no entrance, but there were just as many guards here, ambling up and down the walkway, their gazes sharp on the valleys below. Perhaps Victor had more enemies than just me and my *deirfiúr*.

Light glowed in one of the windows dotting the largest tower. So far, all I'd seen were blacked-out windows. I flew lower to get a look inside, both hopeful and afraid that I'd see Victor.

Pain exploded within me as I slammed straight into an invisible wall. I tumbled in the air, frantically flapping my wings backward, trying to get away from the magical barrier and clear my vision.

I managed to get ahold of myself and caught the wind under my wings again. My gaze darted around, noting that the guards hadn't seemed to see the small bird crashing into the protective shields.

Aidan fluttered below me, no doubt to catch me if I plummeted. Not that I'd fall into the castle. I'd probably just roll down the side of the invisible protective dome. That didn't sound fun either.

I whirled on the wind, having seen enough, and flew back toward our camp. With the moon hidden behind dark clouds, it was difficult to determine my positioning. It took a moment for me to get on the right path, but by the time I did, Aidan was at my side.

I caught sight of our camp and flew to the ground, transforming back to my human form as soon as I landed. I shivered against the chill mountain air as soon as I lost the protection of my feathers, but fortunately I'd transformed with all my clothes. Aidan landed next to me, changing back to human form in a swirl of gray light.

Nix, Del, Connor, Claire, and Emile sat in a circle, perched on rocks that couldn't be comfortable. Del and Claire sharpened their swords while Connor sorted his potion bombs in his specially designed bag.

Emile was at Connor's side. On his shoulder rode Ralph and Rufus, though I noticed Emile was wearing a jacket with two big pockets—one on each breast. It seemed weird until I realized that the pockets were probably designed specifically for Ralph and Rufus. Their battle stations.

Nix looked up. "How'd it go?"

"Fine," I said. "In that I didn't get caught. Otherwise, not great. The place is huge, there are at least sixty demon guards, and there's a protective barrier that will prohibit us from flying in. There's also no visible entrance."

Aidan nodded his agreement, his brow creased with worry lines. "It won't be easy."

"Well, shit," Del said. "Looks like we're doing this the hard way."

"Yep," I said. "Because I have no idea how to get in."

"They must transport in and out," Aidan said. "That's why they've been collecting all the transportation charms."

"Makes sense," Connor said. "So what do we do?"

"Go on foot. See if our Penatrist charms will get us through the barrier, then climb the wall."

"I don't think they're going to work," Aidan said. "His protection spells are the strongest I've ever felt. Even stronger than those on my father's place."

"All we can do is try," I said.

# CHAPTER NINE

Aidan was right. The protection charms on Victor's castle were stronger than even the Penatrist charms could handle.

"Damn it," I muttered as I glared at the one in my hand. "Aren't these things supposed to be infallible?"

Aidan's brow creased as he blinked snowflakes off his eyelashes. "Yes. Whatever is fueling this spell is darker and stronger than anything I've ever encountered."

I shivered against the words and the cold. It'd started snowing as we'd climbed the steep mountainside. How that happened in early September I had no idea, but I took it to be an ill omen.

We'd moved silently through the night, our small herd of seven humans and two rats scrambling up the mountain to the walls of Victor's castle. Now that we were there, it hulked overhead, a dark monstrosity of stone and evil. It glared at us as we searched for a weak spot in the protection shield.

"We've gone halfway around the wall and nothing," Del whispered.

I looked ahead of us, at the long expanse of stone wall that we had yet to search. It wasn't looking good.

Pale, glittering sparkle lights caught my eye down the mountainside, about twenty yards away. They'd appeared twice before this, but I'd thought they were snowflakes glinting in the intermittent moonlight.

"Anyone else see those lights?" I whispered. "Down the mountainside."

As a unit, my friends turned their heads to look.

"Yeah, I noticed them before but thought they were just snow," Del said, her answer mimicking my thoughts so closely that I had to wonder if she hadn't been reading my mind.

"I don't think so," Aidan murmured.

They reminded me of the lights that had guarded the Nullifier's cottage in the Alps, distracting hikers from getting too close. But these weren't quite the same.

"I think they're beckoning," Claire said.

"I'm going to check them out," I said.

"I'm coming with you," Aidan said.

"Us too," Del said.

"No." I shook my head. There wasn't a lot of cover down the mountainside. "You guys stay here, where the guards can't see you. Too many of us away from the wall is asking for them to take notice."

"Fine," Del muttered.

I closed my eyes and called on my magic, reaching for Aidan's signature. Crashing waves and the scent of the forest caught my senses as I mirrored his ability to shift into any animal. Warmth filled my lungs as I turned into a sparrow, my new preference for shifting. I was quick and small in this form, able to sneak around unnoticed.

The world zoomed before me as I shrank and then took off flying. I caught the sound of Aidan's wings flapping behind me as we approached the lights.

They drifted farther away as we neared, and unease prickled my back. Were they trying to lead us from the castle? We couldn't become distracted.

I was about to turn back when they halted in the cover of a stone outcropping, where they were hidden from sight of the castle.

I fluttered to a stop, landing on a big boulder and peering up at the lights. Aidan landed at my side. We didn't shift as we watched the lights glitter brighter. They swirled until they coalesced to form the rough shape of a human.

Magic vibrated on the air, followed by the scent of forest herbs. Something vaguely identifiable. Then it hit me. It smelled a bit like Connor's potions workshop—a jumble of herbs and stones and magic.

A moment later, two slender figures stood before us. They were dressed in dark cloaks, and their skin was so pale that it was nearly translucent. They were skinnier than humans, and their faces had the eerie, otherworldly look of the fae. I couldn't determine their gender from their features, though did it really matter?

The most important thing was that I didn't feel any malice coming from them. If they'd wanted to hurt us, they could have done it already. They'd followed us for at least thirty minutes without us having any idea, I'd wager.

"You can shift," the figure on the left said. I decided the voice was feminine. "It'd be best if we could speak."

The other figure nodded.

I glanced at Aidan. He nodded his head, which looked a bit odd, considering he was a bird, but I trusted his judgment.

I called upon my magic, shifting back to human form in a flash. It was getting easier and easier, thank magic.

"Why did you lead us there?" I asked.

"We want to know your purpose at Vlad's castle."

My brows shot up. "Vlad's castle? As in, Dracula?"

Both figures nodded.

The one on the left spoke. "Yes. This was once his, though it lay abandoned for centuries after his death. What is your purpose here?"

"First, who are you?" I asked. It was one thing that they hadn't attacked us, but I wasn't about to spill my guts until I knew what they wanted.

"I am Aleres, and this is Reofeus. We are shadow sprites who live in this valley."

"We've had many good years here with our clan," Reofeus said. "Until the Dark One arrived."

Twenty bucks that the *Dark One* was Victor Orriodor. I'd go so far as to bet my trove on it.

"We want him gone," Aleres said. "His evil seeps into the valley, poisoning us. But it is our ancestral home. The shadow sprites abandoned this land while Vlad lived here. His evil spread like the Dark One's. After his death, we slowly recolonized this place."

I looked around, wondering if I'd missed something when we'd made our way up through this valley initially. "But I don't see your settlement."

"No, you wouldn't. We don't exist as you do, in boxes for houses." Reofeus shuddered slightly, his dark cloak swaying against the scatter of snow on the ground.

"Why haven't you done anything about it?" I asked. With their ability to float through the air as nothing more than glittering light, they could probably sneak right in.

"We cannot." Aleres reached out his hand as if he would touch the rock next to him. But his hand passed right through.

"That's a problem," Aidan said.

"Not normally." Reofeus frowned. "We have no need to be truly corporeal. But in a circumstance like this, it is a problem. We cannot fight to evict them. We need a champion."

A champion? "Like us?"

"If your goal is to harm the Dark One, which we think it is, then yes. Like you."

"Why do you think we are here to harm him…the Dark One?" Aidan asked.

"You're creeping around like thieves," Reofeus said.

"And we spied on your camp," Aleres said. "If you vow to evict him, we will show you an ancient entrance to the castle. It is far down the mountainside, below the dome of his protection charms. It leads up into the bottom of the castle."

My brows shot up. "But we searched this whole area."

"You searched too close to the castle. The siege bolt-hole is farther away. Even the Dark One does not know it is there."

Oh, jackpot.

"I vow to you that my goal is to destroy him." The words were worthy of a superhero movie, but I meant them. "If we do not succeed today, we will continue until he is gone."

They both nodded, convinced by my vehemence.

"Then retrieve your companions," Aleres said. "And follow us."

Aleres and Reofeus led us far down into the valley.

"You sure about these guys?" Nix whispered.

"Yeah." I stumbled over a rock covered by the thickening snow, cursing the foul weather. "I am. They said there's a siege bolt-hole."

Nix grumbled, but kept up. It made sense that the bolt-hole would be far from the castle to allow residents to escape unnoticed by attacking forces.

Down in the valley, the tree growth thickened. There were still short trees, but they were fat and gnarled like a fairytale forest of old. In the distance, I noticed other faintly glittering lights. Aleres and Reofeus's clan members, perhaps.

We wove our way single file between the tree trunks, skirting the side of the mountain. Finally, Aleres and

Reofeus stopped at an area where the mountainside was particularly overgrown with vines.

"Where is it?" I asked.

Reofeus gestured to the vine-covered wall. "Here. But you must learn how to enter. We do not know how."

*Shit.* I'd really been hoping for an obviously marked door with a nice door handle. Perhaps even a sign that read "Secret Entrance."

No such luck.

Aidan approached the vine-covered wall and ran his hands over it. I joined him, doing the same. Magic sparked beneath my touch, mildly prickly. The door was definitely under here.

I turned to the shadow sprites. "Thank you."

They inclined their heads.

"It is not guarded by the protective charm that covers the rest of the castle because it is so far away," Aleres said. "You should be able to get through if you can determine how to open the door."

I touched the Penatrist charm in my pocket. "We will. Thank you for the help."

"Thank you for yours." Aleres bowed.

Reofeus did the same before they drifted back into the shadows.

I turned toward my friends. "All right. Let's clear off this wall and find the door."

"On it, captain." Connor saluted me.

I punched him lightly on the shoulder, then turned back to the wall and grabbed a handful of the vines. It was oddly slippery as I yanked it away. The vine resisted at first, but I was able to pull it from the wall.

In half a second, another vine grew in its place.

"What the hell!" Del exclaimed.

I glanced at my friends, who were having the same problem. They tugged and yanked, throwing big hunks of vine over their shoulders. But as soon as they pulled the greenery away, more grew in its place.

"We're not going to be able to use the Penatrist charm if we can't find the damned door," Aidan said.

He was right. And this made total sense. Of course a door like this would be hidden from the outside.

Beside me, Emile whispered something to Ralph and Rufus. They leapt out of his pockets and scrambled across the ground, disappearing between the vines.

I nodded after them. "They got a plan?"

Emile nodded.

I stopped tugging at the vines and watched the wall, my gaze scanning back and forth.

Finally, after what felt like ages, a low creaking noise broke the silence. To my left, vines bulged out from the wall, snapping and breaking. A massive wooden door opened outward slowly, revealing a black chasm within.

"Nice," Del said.

"No kidding." I raised my hand, igniting the magic in my lightstone ring to reveal a long corridor leading upward. On the right wall, Ralph and Rufus sat on top of a large lever. They must have pushed it down and opened the door. Below them, dirt spilled from a small hole in the corner of the corridor. They'd dug their way in.

"Good work, guys," I said.

Emile entered the corridor first, shivering slightly as he entered. He stopped, allowing Ralph and Rufus to jump onto his shoulders and scramble down into the big front pockets on his jacket.

I was damned glad that Emile had come along.

Nix hurried into the corridor, hesitating slightly at the entrance, before conjuring two small bits of cheese that she handed to the rats.

"Nicely done," she whispered to them.

Their little noses twitched as they took the cheese with tiny paws.

I stepped into the corridor, hit immediately by a sense of sadness and desperation. It clung to the place, like dark magic or misery that couldn't escape.

"Something bad happened in here," Aidan murmured from beside me. "The place is soaked with it."

"No kidding." Del's voice was nearly soundless. "Vlad was busy in here."

I shined my light all around, noting the scratches in the walls and the dark stains on the floor. I shuddered hard, trying not to imagine what had made those marks and left behind such a sense of misery.

"Let's get going," I said.

"Agreed." Nix grimaced. "I can't get out of here soon enough."

We set off up the corridor, winding our way through a narrow passage studded with boulders and dipping around natural protrusions in the rock. The passage climbed ever higher through the mountain. It must have taken centuries to carve out this escape hatch.

"This goes on forever," Claire muttered a while later. "You sure about this?"

"I think so," I said.

The dark and the cold had nearly drained the strength from me by the time we reached a set of steep stone stairs leading to a ceiling.

"Finally," Del whispered.

I reached out with my magic, feeling for the signatures of other supernaturals. I didn't know where this stairway led, but it'd be just our luck to appear beneath the garrison or something.

But I sensed no magic other than my friends'.

"It's clear," Aidan whispered before he quietly climbed the stairs. At the top, he ducked and placed his hands on the ceiling, slowly pushing upward.

The ceiling didn't give.

He climbed back down and said, "It's not blocked by magic. But I don't want to force it and cause a commotion. If I flip over furniture in the room above, someone might hear."

Del stepped forward, her skin turning blue. "I got this."

It was handy to have a phantom around. She climbed up the stairs and straight into the room above, never ducking her head. My heart pounded as I waited for the trap door to open. Sweat began to trickle down my spine and everything that relied on the success of this mission ping-ponged around in my head.

There were prisoners up there who needed us. Kids, probably. And Victor's arsenal of magical artifacts.

And now Del was up there, too. Possibly captured.

I fidgeted as I glanced around at my friends, all huddled at the end of the corridor. They all looked as nervous as I felt, gazes darting and brows furrowed.

"Do you think she's okay?" Nix whispered.

I didn't have anything good to say, so I didn't say anything at all. I was about to try my comms charm to contact her when a faint cracking noise sounded from above. Then another, and another.

The ceiling shifted as the trap door opened, and Del's transparent blue face peered down.

"All clear," she whispered.

Silently, we climbed up into the little room. Around the entrance to the hatch, the thick wooden floorboards had been torn up.

"Pried them up with my sword," Del said. "Looks like someone redid the floor at some point and hid the escape hatch."

"No wonder Victor never found it," Connor said.

"Our luck," Emile said.

I looked around the room, taking stock of the few items stored down here. A broken chair and mangled broom. A cradle that was nearly falling apart. It was some kind of storage space. There were no windows, which didn't surprise me. We were deep inside the castle at the lowest level.

"Let's go," I whispered, leading the way to the door.

Carefully, I pushed it open, peaking out into the hallway. It was narrow and dark, lined with stone and floored with wood. I stepped out, followed by Emile.

Light, rapid footsteps sounded down the hall and I stiffened. Before I could lunge back into the room, a massive dog appeared at the end of the hall. He was nearly the size of a horse, white with massive brown spots. He halted, his jaw dropping low to reveal large white fangs.

When he raised his head as if to howl, my heart dropped.

Emile stepped forward.

A second later, the hound lowered his head, his dark gaze meeting Emile's.

They were speaking telepathically. Aidan stepped out of the room and joined me, followed by the rest of the gang.

Whatever Emile said to the dog, the animal liked it. It trotted toward us, suddenly not so vicious. It was still huge and bore a striking resemblance to a hellhound, but its eyes were friendly and locked on Emile. The dog smelled of brimstone and flame, so I could check *Met a hellhound* off my list.

"This is Pond Flower," Emile said.

*Pond Flower?* Looked like a Killer to me.

"She chose her own name," Emile added. "The men here call her hound. She doesn't like it."

"Hello, Pond Flower," I said. It was exactly the kind of name I'd expect a dog to choose, though I couldn't say why.

Emile held out a hand for her to sniff, then scratched her head. "She's a guard dog. Along with a dozen others. Though she'd like to live somewhere else."

"Can't say I blame you, Pond Flower," Aidan said.

"We'll help you with that," I told the dog.

Her clever eyes met mine, though I wasn't sure she understood. Beside me, Emile's magic swelled, smelling like grass. A moment later, Pond Flower's tongue lolled out of her mouth in what I would swear was a smile. Emile must have translated for her. I didn't know where the hell I was going to find her and her twelve hellhound siblings a home, but I'd manage.

"Ask her to help us find the FireSouls and the artifacts Victor stole. A chalice, a cauldron, and a gemstone. When we're done, we'll get her out of here."

Emile nodded and turned back to Pond Flower. The dog stared intently up at him, then turned in a tight circle and headed back down the hall, her footsteps clicking on the wood.

"She can take us to the FireSouls, but she doesn't know what the artifacts are or where they're stored."

Fair enough. One out of two wasn't bad, anyway.

We followed in a line, Emile at the front and Claire at the rear. I stuck behind Emile, with Aidan at my back. Every creak of wood beneath my feet or disturbance in the air made me stiffen. We were a massive group of people, just strolling through this castle without a single nook or cranny to hide ourselves in.

I'd like to try to use my power over illusion to conceal us, but it was too risky. Even if I didn't blow us up, my signature might go out of control and alert the guards to my presence. So I did the only thing I could—I crept along behind Emile and tried not to freak out.

Eventually, we reached another staircase. It was only slightly wider than the one leading up to the storage room, though not by much. The stairs were worn down in the middle, the evidence of thousands of feet over hundreds of years. This was definitely an older castle.

Pond Flower padded up the stairs, trailing the scent of brimstone behind her. We stayed close behind her.

The next level of the castle was as barren and creepy as the one below. But if I reached out with my magic, I could just pick up the sense of other supernaturals. Demons, mostly. The smell of smoke accompanied the shadow demons I'd seen earlier on the ramparts, and the unidentifiable signatures of the other species.

We reached a corridor that veered off from the one we were in. Pond Flower turned, heading down that way. In the other direction, a set of stairs led upward. I'd bet anything that Victor kept the artifacts up there, with him. This dungeon basement was too horrible for him to want to hang out in.

"Time to split," I whispered to Aidan.

He nodded. I gestured to my friends, indicating that they should follow Pond Flower and Emile. They nodded and set off, while Aidan and I headed for the stairs.

We'd decided that the larger group would go for the FireSouls, since the prison wouldn't be as heavily occupied as the rest of the castle. It helped that Victor had a habit of using magic rather that live guards to control his prisoners.

Aidan and I were headed for the artifacts, which we assumed were probably stored in a more densely populated part of the castle. A big group would only draw unneeded attention, and if Aidan and I got in a bad way, we could shift and fly away.

I held out a hand and stopped Aidan for a moment, then tried calling on my dragon sense, focusing on the image of the artifacts in my mind. The familiar tug pulled tight around my middle, directing me to the stairs.

*Excellent.* I hadn't been sure if my dragon sense would work inside the protective barrier, but it seemed to. I called upon it again, this time focusing on Victor Orriodor.

I got nothing.

Damn.

He wasn't here. But at least we could still go after the artifacts.

"Up the stairs," I whispered.

We crept upward, finally reaching a level where the air smelled almost fresh. The hall was wider here, but still constructed of roughly hewn stone. A sense of misery still pervaded the space, as if the former occupants' souls still wandered the halls. Ratty tapestries hung listlessly on the walls.

No wonder Victor had chosen to live in his mansion at the waypoint. It was much nicer than this dump.

"We need to head higher up," I whispered.

Ahead of us, a figure stepped out from a doorway.

*Shit!*

I reached for the dagger strapped to my thigh. It was my spare and not enchanted to return to me like my old pair had been, so I had to make this shot count. I didn't want to use my magic as it was too loud and too risky.

The demon opened his mouth to shout as I flung the blade. It sailed end over end, sinking into his throat.

A gurgle escaped his mouth before he collapsed to his knees.

I raced to him, my footsteps silent. Aidan followed, dropping to his knees beside me and turning the body over. I yanked the blade out, making sure the demon was dead—and silent—before patting down his pockets in search of a transportation charm.

I came up with nothing, though it was no surprise. Victor probably rationed them out, giving them only to demons on missions outside of the castle.

"Nothing," I whispered as I rocked back on my heels.

"Then let's go."

I rose and turned back the way we'd come, following the tug around my middle toward the artifacts I sought. As we passed through a shadowy, abandoned great hall, I shivered. Evil lurked in this room more than the rest, like a cloud hanging in the air. What had Vlad done in here? An old drawing that I'd seen flashed in my mind— people impaled on stakes while he calmly ate dinner. Had that happened here?

I'd been wrong about this place. It was perfect for Victor.

We hurried from the room and through several smaller antechambers. Fortunately, the place was blessedly empty. It seemed most of the guards monitored the walls, not the interior of the castle. My heartbeat pounded in my ears, and my muscles were tense, waiting for a demon to jump out at us.

When we reached the spiral staircase that led up toward the artifacts, the comms charm around my neck vibrated with magic. Del's voice drifted out, frantic, though quiet.

"Cass! The alarm is about to be raised. Get out now!"

My stomach dropped. "Do you need help?"

"I think—" The sound of a fight echoed through the charm. "We've got it. But a demon has run off to alert the others. This place is about to go crazy."

*Shit.* "Okay. Get out safe."

Del didn't answer, but I heard more sounds of fighting before the charm cut off. I glanced at Aidan. "We need to hurry."

"Are we close?"

"Yeah." If we got a little lucky, we could make it out of here before anyone saw us. Worst came to worst, we could fly out of the tower windows, so going up was as safe as retreating.

We raced up the spiral staircase. One floor, two, three. I was panting by the time I reached the top, but grateful. The person coming up the stairs always had the disadvantage. I didn't want to be caught there, with demons bearing down upon us.

At the top of the stairs, a dark, deadening feeling swamped me.

"You feel that?" I whispered.

"Yeah."

"The Gundestrop cauldron is definitely up here." My magic was totally repressed—nothing more than ashes in my chest. If there was an ember of power there, I had a hard time feeling it. The cauldron was one of the strongest dampening charms in the world. Maybe *the* strongest.

Without our magic, we were dead meat if the guards found us.

"Let's hurry." I took stock of our surroundings.

We were in a small hallway, with at least six doors extending off of it. This was a damned big castle. My dragon sense no longer worked, so we had to peer into each room as we passed. Fortunately, most of the doors were open. And I was grateful to see no one inside.

But something was eerie about the rooms—even more so than the great hall. By the third room, it hit me.

There were no windows.

*Shit.* That was our escape route.

"Hurry," I said.

We needed to grab the things and make it back down the stairs. At least no one knew we were up here. That should buy us a bit of time.

The door we sought was just ahead. We were so close.

This was the only door that was closed. My hand trembled as I reached for the handle. The protective magic shocked me, making me jerk.

This had to be the room.

Though it looked like the cauldron didn't dampen spells placed on objects—just the magic possessed by a supernatural.

Aidan pulled the Penatrist charm out of his pocket, and I pulled out my own. I hoped they worked, though they should, if the enchantment on the door wasn't affected by the cauldron.

I was about to enter when Aidan gripped my arm.

"Wait," he murmured. He held up the small silver spell stripper and ran it around the edge of the door. "We can enter with the Penatrist charms, but I want to make sure there isn't an alarm on the door."

Smart. We didn't need to direct Victor's guards straight to us.

He finished quickly and tucked the spell stripper back into his pocket. "All clear."

This time, when I reached for the handle, the magic didn't shock me.

I pushed open the door and stepped inside.

The room was so dark that I had to raise my lightstone ring. The yellow glow flared to life in the small room, revealing a set of heavy wooden shelves along the wall. The Gundestrop cauldron sat next to the golden Chalice of Youth. Beside that was the Heartstone, glittering blue and bright.

Aidan moved quickly around the room, running his spell stripper over the shelves and walls, removing any protective enchantments placed on the room.

"Clear," he said.

I hurried forward, reaching for the Heartstone and the chalice. If we just took these two, we'd stay fast and mobile but also put a real dent in Victor's plans.

I grabbed them from the shelf, catching sight of a flash of silver metal beneath each of them just as sirens blared to life.

*Shit!* Victor had put *human* security measures in place? As soon as I'd taken the artifacts off the weight sensors, the alarms had blared to life. I'd never expected him to use human security.

Half a second later, four demons appeared in the room, their massive forms filling the darkened space. A heavy body slammed into me, throwing me to the ground. The Heartstone and chalice flew from my grip, clattering into the far corner where a demon swooped down to pick them up.

*Damn it!*

My magic was still ashes inside my chest. All I had were the daggers at my thighs, and the odds weren't looking good. Aidan and I couldn't even shift to get out of here.

The heavy body on top of mine was shoved aside. Aidan's big hand grabbed my arm and pulled me up.

The demons stood opposite the door. Four more demons appeared.

"Run for it," I said.

We whirled to escape, but more demons waited in the hall.

They closed in on us, all shapes and sizes. Shadow demons, the fire sword demons, and two I didn't recognize.

I wanted to draw my daggers, but they weren't enchanted to return to me like my other pair, so I'd be chucking away my only weapon. Instead, I reached deep for my magic, praying that I could access even a little of it despite the cauldron's effects.

It sparked to life inside my chest, a tiny ember. I fanned the flame, pulling the magic from deep inside of me and calling upon my gift of lightning.

While I did so, Aidan drew his own pair of daggers and surged into the crowd of demons blocking the exit, slashing and stabbing.

When the lightning cracked and burned beneath my skin, I released a jet at the nearest demon. Thunder boomed as it cracked toward him, but it was a puny bolt. Not even enough to kill.

The demon shook and dropped, and I built up my magic again, letting the lightning crackle and grow inside of me.

There was a lake of power within me that I could access only with a straw.

A demon lunged for me and I dodged, but the bite of steel cut into my arm. I gasped at the fiery pain as I threw a bolt of lightning at a demon near the exit.

As it slammed into him, another demon leapt toward me, swinging his fire sword in a great arc. I barely managed to dodge the burning blade, but another struck me in the back, slicing across my shoulder.

Beside me, Aidan had felled three demons, but there were still a dozen more now. Only a few seconds had passed, and we were already screwed. I didn't have enough of my power, and there were too many of them, with more appearing every second.

We were trapped.

This was the end of us.

I'd fight 'til I died, but I would die here.

"Do not kill them!"

My skin froze at the sound of the voice. I glanced over my shoulder, dread crawling up from the pit of my stomach.

Victor Orriodor stood in the center of the room, having just transported here. His dark gaze was gleeful as he looked at me. It was the most emotion I'd ever seen in him. Normally, he just looked like a bored banker, with the bland haircut and suit to match.

Despite the Gundestrop cauldron's dampening power, his evil flowed out from him like a dark fog.

Oh, we were dead meat. No matter what he said.

The only positive was that Victor didn't have his powers. Or did he?

I glanced at Aidan, and his gaze said the same thing I was thinking.

*Run.*

Even if it was hopeless, we had to run.

I turned back to the demons blocking our escape and fought with everything I had. I drew my dagger because my magic was just too slow. I sliced and stabbed, more savage than I'd ever been. But within seconds, a massive demon had his arms clamped around my middle. He squeezed so hard I dropped my daggers, but I thrashed and kicked.

It did no good. It was like being trapped in a stone wall.

Beside me, Aidan staggered beneath the weight of two demons who tried to drag him to the ground. Their muscled gray arms bulged as they gripped him, but Aidan was a huge man. It would take more than two demons.

Others rushed forward, intent on overpowering Aidan. My heart threatened to explode from my chest.

All was lost. We couldn't fight over a dozen demons without our powers. Not with measly daggers.

A brilliant red bird zoomed by my face, plowing into one of the demons clinging to Aidan. The demon burst into flames and howled, staggering back. A blue blur flew at my face. It dodged me at the last minute, exploding against the head of the demon who gripped me from behind.

Icy water rained down on me as the demon choked and gagged, drowning in the water.

The dragonets!

The stone dragonet smashed into the other demon gripping Aidan, his little brown form packing the punch of a cannon ball. The gray demon was thrown back against the stone wall.

Aidan raced toward me. We had to run for it. The way was clear for just a moment.

Not long enough.

The other demons surged forward, blocking the way. The dragonets could help, but they weren't enough. I didn't care. I'd go down fighting so hard they'd have to kill me to get me out of this tower.

I grabbed my daggers from the ground just as the strangest clattering sound came from the round stairs. A half second later, the massive form of Pond Flower appeared in the hall. Her eyes blazed with flame, and her muzzle was pulled back from her teeth, revealing glinting white fangs. The smell of brimstone was so strong I almost gagged.

Behind her, more hellhounds appeared from the stairs. Black and brown, all as big as Pond Flower and all with flame-red eyes.

They charged.

My heart leapt into my throat, but they passed by me, headed straight for the demons. They bowled over the demon nearest me, opening the way for my escape.

"Thank you!" I cried.

Aidan lunged to my side. The hounds set up a barrier between us and the demons. An eerie black flame rose up from their fur, creating a wall. Why their magic worked here, I had no idea. Perhaps because they were animals. Or their magic was fueled by hell, something that had no basis on Earth.

I didn't hang around to ponder why. I wasn't an idiot enough to look a gift hound in the mouth.

Aidan and I ran for it, sprinting down the hall and the spiral staircase. The stairs were so old and uneven that I nearly fell three times.

By the time we made it to the bottom, the strange clattering sound came from the stairs again.

Hellhound nails on the stone, I realized. They were retreating.

"Go!" Aidan shouted.

We raced through the corridor and out into the great hall. There were demons in there now. Shadow demons, from the look of them.

They hurled smoke bombs at us as we raced through the great hall. I dodged one, but was caught by another. Pain flared at my back as the smoke bomb plowed into me. I flew forward onto my front, barely managing to break my fall with my hands.

Aidan grabbed my arm and pulled. I scrambled up off the stone floor and glanced behind me. The hellhounds charged across the great hall, fleeing the mass of demons behind them.

Our pursuers hurled smoke bombs and fireballs. They exploded all around, bouncing off the hellhounds' thick hides. But Aidan and I weren't protected by the same magic.

We turned to flee. We just had to make it outside or to a window. From there, we could shift and fly away.

But there were no windows in this whole magic-forsaken castle. If we couldn't make it to one, escape was impossible.

Del burst into the great hall from the other side of the room. The smoke dragonet was just ahead of her.

Leading her to us.

Her gaze widened as she caught sight of us, chased by hellhounds and demons. She sprinted harder, her dark hair flying behind her. When a smoke bomb nearly hit her, she turned into her phantom form, her skin glinting blue.

She collided with us, wrapping her incorporeal arms around Aidan and me, ready to transport us away. Her touch shocked my skin, but I'd take more than a little shock to get us out of here.

"Not without the hounds!" I yelled.

Her startled gaze met mine. "I don't think I can take so many!"

The hounds were almost upon us now, only feet away. They gathered around, pressing close in a huddle.

"Try!" I cried.

The demons were almost upon us. Del clenched her eyes shut, and I felt the ether pull us in, sucking us through space.

When I opened my eyes, we stood on the tarmac at the tiny airport. The thirteen hellhounds were gathered around us, panting and smelling of brimstone.

We'd made it.

# CHAPTER TEN

"This is the weirdest plane ride of my life," I said.

I was still partially shell shocked from our near escape. We'd all made it out of Victor's castle, though barely, and were hurtling into the sky in Aidan's jet.

"So you got them all?" I asked my friends.

Every one of my friends had bruises or cuts, but their gazes were bright with victory.

"Yeah," Nix said. "Three boys."

I glanced toward the back of the plane. Emile was sitting with them, Ralph and Rufus on his shoulders. The boys looked to be about twelve and were skinny and pale. But they looked happy, surrounded by all thirteen of the hellhounds, who lounged on the floor. Actually, we were all surrounded by hellhounds. The huge dogs took up every bit of floor space in the plane.

Which smelled like brimstone.

At least we'd been partially successful. And no one had been killed, which was a small miracle.

"How did you transport so many hellhounds?" Connor asked Del. "I thought you could only take a couple people at a time."

"And why did you?" Claire asked.

"Pond Flower and her friends saved us," I said. "And we promised her a new life."

Claire glanced at the dogs doubtfully, clearly wondering where we were going to keep thirteen dogs who weighed at least two hundred pounds each and looked like they came from hell. Which they had.

"But how did you manage, Del?" Claire asked.

Del had been silent until now, her gaze alternately shocked and thoughtful. "I uh, felt strong when they touched me, I guess. Normally, transporting drains me. It's why I can only take a couple people—that's all the juice I have. But the hounds felt like part of me. It was so easy to take them along."

Pond Flower, who sat at Del's feet, pressed herself against her side and gazed at her adoringly.

"Holy shit," Nix said, realization in her voice. "It's because you're Death. And those hounds are from hell. Death. Hell. Get it?"

She nodded slowly. "Yeah, I think you're right."

Okay, wow. That was a revelation.

"So are they your dogs now?" Claire asked.

I glanced at the dogs. With the exception of Pond Flower, the rest were piled around the boys.

"I think they're theirs." I hiked a thumb at the boys.

Del nodded. "Yeah, I agree. I'm not a hellhound whisperer or anything."

"They turned on Victor quickly," Aidan said.

"They didn't like him," Emile said.

We'd reached our cruising altitude, and he'd come up to the front to join us. I glanced back to see the boys asleep on the couches, the dogs piled around him.

"Pond Flower here says they were sold to him by some demons," Emile continued. "They didn't like him, but they didn't know where else to go. Once we came, they saw a better opportunity and took it."

"They saved our life," I said.

"Yes," Emile said. "Hellhounds have rare powers. They make excellent guard dogs because of their black flame. No one can touch it or pass through it without their permission."

"We saw that," Aidan said. "They turned into strange torches and stopped the demons. But the Gundestrop cauldron didn't affect them the way it did the other supernaturals. They still had their powers."

Emile nodded. "They don't get their power in the way other supernaturals do. They're fueled by the powers of hell. As long as hell exists, so do the hellhounds and their powers."

"Thank magic for that. And for Pond Flower." I reached down and scratched her ears.

"Yes. Ralph and Rufus have quite taken to her." The rats jumped off his shoulders and sat on Pond Flower, who didn't seem to mind. "I think she named herself for a water lily. I saw the image in my head when she told me her name."

"It suits her," Aidan said.

Nix grinned, then held out her hands. Her magic flowed on the air, smelling like flowers and feeling like a fresh breeze. A moment later, a broad white flower sat in her palms.

A water lily.

Pond Flower made a huffing noise of approval, her dark gaze bright on the flower.

"This is you, huh?" Nix asked.

After the stress of the last few days, watching Nix hold the lily so that Pond Flower could sniff it was easily the highlight of my week.

"We're going to need to find a home for them," I said.

"I don't think the pound takes hellhounds," Connor said.

Del stared at him, aghast. "As if we'd turn them over to the pound!"

Connor raised his hands. "Sorry, sorry! A bad joke."

"What about the League of FireSouls?" Nix asked. "We're going to ask them to help us find the boys' families. What about taking the dogs as well? That place they live in is huge and basically empty. Plenty of room to run around. And the whole Arcadian forest for them to enjoy."

"Good idea," I said. When we'd visited a few weeks ago, the place had been beautiful but far too big for the FireSouls who lived there. "We could even pay for their food, if necessary."

"I think it might be," Del said. "Look at the size of them."

"It won't be necessary," Emile said. "They survive off of magic. Fire is an occasional treat for them."

"It's settled then. We ask the League of FireSouls for help with the boys and the dogs." Our team was much bigger than I'd ever expected it to be.

"How did you make it out of the castle with the boys?" Aidan asked.

"The old-fashioned way," Claire said. "Fighting."

"Then we ran for it," Connor said. "We just had to make it to the car. We were nearly there when the smoke dragonet came back for Del."

"They're always there when I need them," I said. "Like they have a sixth sense where I'm concerned."

"Did they get out okay?" Aidan asked.

"Yes. I'm sure." I rubbed my chest, wincing at the pull and sting of my wounds. "I think I'd feel it if something happened to them. And in every other circumstance, they were fine."

"But you didn't get the artifacts?" Nix asked.

"No. We never stood a chance. That bastard installed modern alarms in the room where he stored his stuff."

"In that old place?" Del asked.

"Yep. He was taking no chances."

"Wow. I really wouldn't have expected that," Nix said.

"Neither did I," I said. "But we're going to need a new plan now."

"We'll think of something," Del said.

I hoped she was right. Because we had to.

Roughly five hours later, I was squished into the backseat of Aidan's Range Rover next to Phillip, one of the FireSoul boys, as we drove through the Highlands toward Aidan's land.

He'd just woken from a long snooze pressed against the window, so I asked, "How're you doing?"

He rubbed his eyes and looked at me. His dark hair was floppy and dirty, and his gaze looked older than it should have. "All right, I guess."

"Yeah?" I could try to cheer him up by reminding him that he was free, but that would be pretty much the worst direction I could go with this.

He nodded. "Yeah. I'm glad we're not in that place anymore, but I don't know where my parents are."

My heart twisted in my chest for him. I'd lived through everything he had, so I had a pretty good idea what he was going through.

"I know," I said. "And I understand if you're scared about that. But I promise that we're going to help you find them."

"What if they aren't alive?"

"Then we'll help you with that as well."

For a second, his chin trembled and it looked like he was going to cry, but he stiffened his back and nodded. "Okay."

This was one tough kid. I hated to think of the circumstances that had made him tough. Unfortunately, I knew all too well.

"You know," I said, then hesitated, wondering how to phrase my thoughts. "I was, uh, once in your position. Locked up by Victor Orriodor, I mean."

"Really?" He shot me a skeptical look.

"Yeah. When I was fourteen and fifteen. It's how I met Del and Nix." Memories pushed at my mind, miserable, horrible ones. I shoved them aside and tried to get my words out. "What I'm trying to say is, that everything worked out in the end. It'll work out for you too."

He gave me a doubtful look that broke my heart.

"If it helps any, I'm going to kill the guy who locked you up."

His gaze brightened at my bloodthirsty statement. I'd had a feeling it might.

"Yeah?" he asked.

"Oh yeah. He doesn't stand a chance."

"Good," he said.

"Do you know anything about why he kept you locked up?"

He shook his head. "I think he wanted us because we are FireSouls, but I don't know any more."

"It's okay," I said.

Del and Nix were talking to the two other boys, so hopefully they figured something out.

We turned onto the road that led us to Aidan's land and I said, "Almost there."

"Good," Phillip said.

Ten minutes later, we arrived, dirty and exhausted. It was nearly noon, though it felt far later, and the lot of us were ready for a meal and a nap. A twelve-hour nap.

Unfortunately, there were seven adults, three children, and thirteen hellhounds. Aidan's house had only one tiny bathroom and two bedrooms. But still, it was the safest place for us until we could ask the League of FireSouls to take the boys and try to reunite them with their families.

We all piled out of the car and waited impatiently while he disarmed the protection charms. The hellhounds set off running, frolicking through the woods. He'd had to call and arrange a massive truck to bring them all here.

"The League of FireSouls should be here in a little while," I told the boys while we walked inside. I'd called Corin, my contact with the League, and explained the situation to her. "They're going to help you find your families."

*If they're still alive.* It was very possible their families weren't still alive, but saying so would *not* help the situation.

"How about I get us some food, eh?" Connor asked the boys.

They'd eaten piles of peanuts and pretzels on the plane, but they all nodded eagerly anyway. I didn't blame them. They hadn't yet had a decent meal. And after I'd escaped the Monster as a kid, all I'd wanted to do was eat, too.

While Connor got the boys some food, I walked to the sagging couch and collapsed onto it. My whole body ached, cuts and bruises flaring to life now that my adrenaline had faded. The cuts on my back and arm were shallow, I thought, but they still stung like a bitch. I probably should ask Aidan to see to them, but he'd gone back to the border of his land to wait for the League of

FireSoul emissaries to arrive. In order for them to pass through the protective barriers, he needed to be present.

Del and Nix joined me on the sofa. They looked as worn out as I felt, but we needed to talk about what we'd learned when we'd each talked to a different boy.

"So," Nix said. "Did either of yours know anything about Victor's plans for them?"

"Not Phillip," I said.

"Martin said that they were being trained to be thieves," Del said. "He'd been there almost a year."

"A slave. Like Aaron," I said, remembering the FireSoul I'd met earlier this summer. He'd been enslaved by Victor, set loose only to find artifacts that Victor desired. "At least they hadn't been collared."

"Thank magic," Del said.

"And at least Victor didn't have a more sinister plan for them," Nix said.

"No, I think he's saving that for us." I scrubbed a hand over my face.

"There could be more FireSoul slaves out there," I said. "Not locked up, but out on assignments for Victor."

"Well, then we need to kill him, don't we?" Del said. "When he dies, their collars will pop off and they'll be free."

I nodded, remembering the slave collar I'd worn and how it'd popped off when I'd killed the Shifter woman who'd owned it—and me, as long as I'd been wearing it.

Just one more good reason to kill Victor Orriodor.

When the door to the cabin creaked open and Aidan walked in, leading Corin and Alton, I almost collapsed with gratitude. We were that much closer to taking a nap.

I rose, every inch of me aching, to greet the two emissaries from the League of FireSouls. Alton, a handsome black man who wore a warrior's leather armor, and Corin, a slender blonde woman in matching armor, smiled when they saw me.

"Aidan explained that you rescued three FireSouls from Victor Orriodor's headquarters," Corin said.

I nodded. "Yeah. We were hoping you'd take them and try to reunite them with their families. As long as Victor and the Council are after me and my *deirfiúr*, it's not safe for them with us."

Not to mention the fact that I had no idea what to do with three kids.

"And, ah, there's a few hellhounds who need a home," Del said. "We thought they might be happy at the League headquarters. It's so large and empty. They'd be great company!"

Corin grinned. "Really trying to sell it, eh?"

Del shrugged. "We don't really have room for thirteen hellhounds."

Alton's brows shot up. "Thirteen?"

"Yes, but they're all lovely," Del said. "I can vouch for them."

"How?" Corin asked.

"I have a connection with them somehow, though I don't entirely understand it. They're good dogs. And good protectors. They'll be an asset."

Alton nodded. "Fine. We'll take them. The place could use some livening up."

I thought sadly of how abandoned the beautiful castle compound had been—like some fairytale that had been trapped in time. The League had once been much larger. Until the majority of them, my poor parents included, had been killed trying to rescue me and my *deirfiúr* from Victor.

"Thanks," I said.

Del grinned broadly. She really liked the dogs, but she was right. Hellhounds wouldn't be happy living in our apartments and going on walks on city sidewalks.

From outside, a happy howl echoed, as if Pond Flower knew she'd found a good home.

"So, we've got three boys and thirteen hellhounds," Corin said. "Anything else?"

"Yes." I nodded to the table near the kitchen. "Want a seat? Because I sure could use one."

We found seats at the rough wooden table while Connor got the boys settled on the couch with plates of sandwiches. When he joined us, the whole gang was crowded around. Connor, Claire, Emile, Nix, Del, Aidan, Alton, Corin, and myself.

"We're going to need help," I said. Because it probably wasn't coming from the Alpha Council.

"Possibly a lot of it," Aidan added.

"What kind?" Corin asked.

I explained to them the situation with the Alpha Council and Victor—that he wanted vengeance and whatever method he chose would probably result is massive loss of life.

Alton nodded slowly. "You can count on us to help when you call. Do you have a plan?"

"No," I said.

"Not even a little bit," Del added.

Aidan leaned forward, his gaze serious. "But we will."

"Let us know when you do," Corin said. "In the meantime, we'll take the boys and try to find their families."

Relief flowed through me at the words. We had what we needed.

And it was finally time for a nap.

By the time I'd said goodbye to the boys, Pond Flower, and her dozen siblings, I was actually staggering. It wasn't even dark yet, but everyone was so beat we were going to crash early, then get a jumpstart tomorrow.

Nix had conjured mattresses for Connor, Claire, and Emile out in the living room. She and Del would share the other bedroom. That left Aidan and me in this one.

"I could sleep for twelve hours," Aidan said.

"Likewise." I winced as I peeled off my leather jacket. My back burned with the movement.

"What the hell, Cass?" Aidan's concerned voice broke through the hazy pain in my head.

I turned to see his concerned gaze glued to me. "Huh?"

"The back of your shirt is soaked with blood."

"Yeah. Probably." My jacket must have covered it.

Aidan stepped around me. I couldn't feel or see him, but I knew he was inspecting the wound. His big hand reached down and pulled my dagger from the thigh holster. My shirt tugged and pulled as he cut the rest of it off me. I couldn't help sagging in relief. Trying to get the shirt off the normal way would have hurt like hell.

"This is deep," he said.

"Nah." Though it did really hurt now.

"I'll take care of it."

His fingertips brushed my back gently, just above the wound. Warmth flowed from his hand into me, bringing with it a relief from the pain.

"You're amazing," I murmured.

"I know." He stepped to my side and inspected the cut on my arm. "This one isn't as bad, but let me get it."

I stood there like a mannequin, letting him care for me. It was freaking great. I was used to taking care of myself, but this kind of thing was nice.

"Anything else I'm not seeing?" Aidan asked when he was done healing me.

I shook my head. The sound of the shower cut off. "I think it's my turn."

"Our turn," Aidan said. "We'll save water."

"Save water, eh?" I tried to give him a goofy, sexy eyebrow wiggle.

He grinned. "Mostly I just think you need help standing up."

A weak laugh escaped me. "Yeah, I probably do."

He rubbed his hand gently over my hip, nudging me toward the door. "Let's go, champ."

I was only in my bra and jeans as I peeked out into the little hallway, but I didn't care. I wanted to be in the shower about three hours ago.

Nix was just leaving, her hair wrapped in her ducky towel from home. "All yours."

"Thanks." I darted into the little bathroom, which was filled with steam. Aidan crowded in behind me.

We showered quickly, both of us stuffed into the tiny shower stall. I leaned against him and let him wash my hair, marveling again at my good fortune.

By the time we made it into the little bed, we were clean and dry. I curled up against Aidan, my head on his shoulder, and draped my arm over his chest. His big hand played idly with my damp hair.

"You know, you're the best thing that's ever happened to me," Aidan murmured.

"Yeah?"

"Yeah. And I love you."

I glanced up at him, my eyes wide. I wasn't so tired anymore.

"What?" I said dumbly.

The corner of his mouth tugged up as he looked town at me. "You heard me. I love you."

My heart scrambled around in my chest, trying to figure out what to do. This was not a drill! Joy and panic surged through me. No one other than Nix or Del or my parents had ever told me they loved me. Love was a *big deal*. It was a life changer.

"I, uh—" My gaze darted around the room.

"Don't worry, Cass." His voice was warm and calm. "I didn't say it expecting you to say it back."

I didn't know what to say. I didn't know how to say it. So I gripped him harder around the chest, not wanting him to get up. But there was no tension in his body.

"It's okay, Cass. Really. I'm not saying it to get anything out of it. Not even you saying it in return. But with everything going on, it was time to tell you. We don't know what tomorrow will bring, and I wanted you to know. To know that I'm in your corner one hundred percent."

Tears burned my eyes, and I looked up at him. "You know that thing you said about me being one of the best things to ever happen to you?"

"Yeah."

"Likewise."

He grinned, so handsome that it made my heart ache. "I know. And when this is all over, we've got a future together. A good one."

That was the best news I'd heard all week. Hell, all year.

# CHAPTER ELEVEN

I woke to the smell of bacon and coffee. When I opened my eyes and saw that I was still in the little bedroom at Aidan's place, I thought I had to be dreaming the scents. As far as I knew, all we had in the house were sandwich supplies and beer. Which, honestly, didn't sound so bad.

But bacon and coffee in the morning sounded even better.

I rolled over to find Aidan, but he was already out of bed. Memories of what he'd told me last night flashed through my mind.

How the hell had I gotten so lucky? I'd even mucked it up after he'd told me, stuttering and not saying it back, and he'd still been cool with it.

A grin spread over my face as I climbed out of bed. A full night's sleep had done me wonders. Combined with Aidan's revelation, I felt like a million bucks. We could handle this. Whatever Victor tried to throw at us, we could handle.

Especially if we had bacon and coffee. And I'd figure out how to tell Aidan how I really felt. Without stuttering.

I dressed quickly and made my way out into the main living area. Everyone else was up, though just recently from the looks of them. Connor and Claire were in the kitchen, being the best friends in the world and whipping up an amazing breakfast of eggs and bacon.

Emile was leaning against the counter, drinking a cup of coffee, while Ralph and Rufus sat next to him gnawing on a huge hunk of cheese.

"Hey, Sleeping Beauty." Nix handed me a cup of coffee.

I inhaled the scent, energized. "Did I sleep too long?"

"Nah," Del said. It's only five thirty. We've got plenty of time left today to beat the bad guys."

"Excellent."

Aidan stepped up behind me and pressed a kiss to my head. I leaned back against him, comfort and happiness filling me. Sometime soon, we'd face the battle of a lifetime against Victor. But for now, things were good.

"Food's up!" Connor called.

We all gathered round, taking plates and filling up with eggs and bacon. It was the weird British kind, sorta like Canadian bacon, but it smelled good. It was a tight fit around the table, but we managed.

I'd shoveled down half my plate by the time Aidan said, "We need a plan."

"True story," Del said.

"I'm going to call Elenora, the leader of the Alpha Council," Aidan said. "I'll plead our case again. See if they see reason."

"We can only hope," Nix said.

"While you call Elenora, I'll practice my magic a bit," I said.

"We'll come help you," Del said.

"No way." I shook my head. "Too dangerous."

"Aidan told us how last time you just knocked him over," Nix said. "So you're clearly getting better. It'll be fine."

"Still..."

"No arguments," Del said. "We're running out of time. Shit is going to get real faster than we expect. You're going to need the full force of your magic soon, and you're not going to be alone in a calm environment when you need it. Better to practice with people around. Real life scenario kinda shit."

She had a point. I didn't have ages to get my magic under control. More than likely, this was the last chance I'd have.

"And distractions might be good for you," Claire said. "It'll keep you from overthinking."

"Oh, all right," I said. "Nix and Del, you can come along."

"Excellent," Del said.

We finished eating and headed out. Connor, Claire, and Emile stayed to clean up. They were all going to work on creating more potion bombs for Emile, using things found in the forest.

162

Nix, Del, and I tugged on jackets before stepping out into the cool morning air. Birds chirped their morning songs as we made our way through the woods to the clearing where I liked to practice.

"So, uh, something happened last night," I said.

"Yeah?" Nix asked.

"Yeah. Aidan told me he loved me."

"No shit, Sherlock," Del said. "'Course he loves you."

I socked her in the shoulder and she grinned. "Did you say it back?"

"No."

"Idiot!" Nix said.

"I wasn't sure!"

"'Course you're sure!" Del said. "I've seen how you look at him. And speaking of looking at him—meow. You picked a hot one."

"I didn't really pick him," I said. "It just kinda… happened."

"However it happened, I'm happy for you," Nix said.

Del started humming the wedding march, and I punched her again.

She grinned. "Touchy, touchy."

We reached the clearing, thank magic, and could stop talking about Aidan. Though they were right. I probably did love him.

Del's gaze traveled around the disturbed dirt and the torn off tree limbs. "You do all this?"

"Yeah." I nodded. "This is what we call me having control."

"So you do need some practice, I guess," Nix said.

"Maybe we'll stand back a bit."

"Ten yards, at least," I said.

They stepped back into the tree line. Dappled sunlight lit up the ground around us, turning the place into a fairy glen. I rubbed my fingertips over the wide gold dampening cuff on my wrist.

"Okay, I don't think I should start with lightning," I said.

Del nodded emphatically. "Agreed."

"I'm going to try mirroring Nix's conjuring powers," I said. "Cool, Nix?"

"Yeah. Try to make a car. That's *way* hard. Even I can't do that."

Nix did have trouble with complex mechanical items. All conjurers did.

"All right." I pulled off the cuff and tossed it to the ground, almost staggering from the power that flowed through me.

"Whoa there, tiger," Del muttered. "You're strong."

"Try to dampen your signature," Nix said. "I'd be able to feel you from a mile away."

I sucked in a deep breath and tried to gather up my magic, shoving it down deep inside of me. I'd still have access to it, but hopefully no one else would be able to sense it. My skin prickled from the effort and my head buzzed a bit, but I felt more in control. Contained. Almost like a bottle of soda that'd been shaken up.

I just needed to not lose control, or I'd blast magic everywhere. We'd seen where that had gotten me.

"Nice," Del said. "I don't feel you at all anymore."

"Same," Nix said. "Now make us a car!"

A tiny grin tugged at my mouth as I pictured my old junker, Cecilia. She wasn't impressive, but I was most familiar with her and that would help.

I tried to keep control of my magic as I reached out for Nix's signature. After a few moments, the taste of vanilla exploded on my tongue and the scent of flowers seeped into me.

*Got it.* From there, it wasn't hard to pull her talent toward me, to borrow it and manipulate it. I fed it my power, envisioning creating Cecilia from nothing.

I didn't often mirror Nix's conjuring gift because it was a difficult one that took a lot of practice. Better to let the experts do it. But I needed to gain control.

My fingertips tingled as I tried to build Cecilia. The clearing in front of me sparkled with light as my magic swirled on the air. Slowly, the shadowy form of a car appeared. It was transparent and looked slightly misshapen, but it was definitely a car.

Magic vibrated in my chest as I tried to perfect it. But my vision began to blur. Black crept in at the edges. My heart raced. What was happening?

"Quit screwing with our vision, Cass!" Del called.

That wasn't me! I didn't mean to!

I tried to pull myself back from the magic, shut it off. I was losing control in a totally new way. But I couldn't escape. The black closed farther in on my vision as another magical signature began to fill the air.

What the hell was happening?

Was someone coming? I was almost blind.

Panic cut the last hold I had on my magic. It burst out of me, an explosion of light. I did everything I could to keep it inside of me, like a sneeze I didn't want to let loose.

I stumbled backward onto my butt. Through my hazy vision, I saw Del and Nix on the ground as well, but they looked okay.

"Why the hell can't you stay on your feet? Is walking new to you?" a sharp feminine voice said.

I shook my head, trying to clear my vision. But instead of the clearing, two figures appeared in my mind's eye. As I blinked, they became superimposed on the forest.

"Mordaca? Aerdeca?" I asked.

"Who else?" Aerdeca said. She looked just as perfect and put together as usual, even in my vision. Her slender form was draped in one of her favored white suits, and her ice-blond hair flowed straight down her back.

"They're a bit simple." Her sister Mordaca arched a dark brow. Her usual plunging black Elvira dress looked out of place in the forest. So did her bouffant black hair and dark, winged eye makeup.

They looked like they were standing in the middle of the clearing. To their side, Del and Nix stood, dusting leaves off their pants. They didn't look any worse for wear. I climbed easily to my feet as well, grateful I hadn't done us any damage when I'd lost control of my magic. It'd been a minor slip, even smaller than the one before.

"What are you doing here?" Del asked.

"And how?" Nix gestured around. "You can't get through Aidan's barriers."

"We know." Aerdeca elegantly crossed her arms in front of her chest. "We're not actually here. We're visions inside your mind."

I blinked and squinted, trying to follow what she was saying. But she was right. Even though she kinda looked like she was here, she wasn't. Not really.

"Nice gift," I said.

Aerdeca tilted her head toward her sister. "It's Mordaca's."

"I'm very talented." Mordaca's blood-red lips curled up in a confident smile.

I grinned back. Mordaca was cocky, but I liked it. I didn't like how women were expected to apologize for their accomplishments and practice extreme modesty. Mordaca was on the far opposite end of that, but it made me like her even more.

Even though I was pretty sure she didn't like me.

"Why are you here?" I asked.

"Aethelred had another vision." Mordaca's smoky voice was sharp. "A bad one. Ever since your last visit, he's been scrying for you. He's finally seen something."

"What?" I asked.

"When you confront your enemy, one of the Triumvirate will fall, only to rise again."

My skin chilled, and my stomach dropped. "What the hell does that mean?"

"That one will die?" Aerdeca looked uncomfortable saying it. "I don't really know."

"But we'll rise again? Like Lazarus? Or a zombie?" Del asked.

"I don't want to be a zombie," Nix said.

I was feeling vaguely ill. Seers couldn't see all, but what they could see always came true. One of us would fall? That sounded terrible.

"This is all fated," Mordaca said. "There is no escaping it."

"So what can we do about it?" Del demanded. "Because at this point, it just seems that you're here to deliver bad news. It's not exactly helpful."

"Of course it is." Aerdeca's voice was sharp. "I'm sorry to be the bearer of bad tidings, but quit complaining and use what we're giving you. And I do have information that might help. Aethelred said that you must find what Victor seeks on Alpha Council land."

"Where on their land?" Del asked.

"He wants something that is under Glencarrough. Perhaps to help him destroy the Shifters, or for his own purposes."

"*Under* Glencarrough?" I asked.

Mordaca nodded. "That is what he said. Under. There is an entrance through an ancient broch east of Glencarrough."

I hadn't seen a broch when we'd approached the stronghold by car. The Iron Age stone towers were often at least twenty feet tall, so I'd have noticed. It must be in the woods.

"How do we find it?" I asked. "That's a lot of land to cover."

"Go there and you will have help." Aerdeca shrugged. "At least, that's what Aethelred said."

"*All* he said," Mordaca added. "That's all we've got."

It'd have to be enough.

"And you can count on our assistance should you need it," Aerdeca said. "Aethelred explained what was at stake."

"Thank you." Before the words were entirely out of my mouth, Aerdeca and Mordaca disappeared.

My vision cleared immediately, and I staggered slightly, suddenly alone in my mind again.

"Weird," Del said.

I looked at them. Del was rubbing her temples, and Nix was blinking hard.

"I don't think I like that kind of impromptu visit," Nix said.

"Me neither." I approached them, grabbing my golden cuff off the ground and putting it on as I walked. "And I don't like what they told us."

Nix grimaced. "Yeah, that sounded a lot like one of us would die."

My skin chilled again, and it had nothing to do with the early morning breeze.

"But she said we would rise again," Del said.

"I don't know about you guys, but I sure don't feel immortal," I said.

"No, you're right." Del frowned. "We can't focus on that now. Just on what needs to be done. It sounds like the greater power he seeks is underground. Accessed only through the broch."

"Yeah." I was glad to have a direction. "Let's go tell the others."

As we left, I glanced at the clearing behind me. My practice had been going well. Perhaps I'd snag another few hours later today, but right now, at least I wasn't injuring my friends while using it.

# CHAPTER TWELVE

No one liked hearing the news we had to share, least of all Aidan. While I'd been practicing my magic, he'd called the Alpha Council, and they'd agreed to speak to him again, but only in person.

"I think we should check out the broch first," I said. We all sat around the kitchen table in Aidan's cottage, coffee steaming away in mugs in front of us. "They could still imprison you for associating with a known FireSoul, so if you're going to speak with them in person, you're better off having more information on your side."

"I agree," Aidan said. "And the broch is on the way to Glencarrough. We'll check there first, then I'll meet with them on neutral ground, outside of the stronghold."

"Smart," I said. I hadn't liked the idea of him walking into their fortress again.

"We can leave soon, if it works for everyone," Del said. "I really think we need to move quickly on this."

Everyone nodded. I stood and said, "I'm going to call Dr. Garriso and see if he can give me a better idea of where the broch is. He has maps of almost all the archaeological sites in Britain."

I left everyone to gather up their things and went into the bedroom to call. I had to plug in my cell just to get some battery, and once the screen flared to life, I punched in the numbers.

Dr. Garriso answered on the fourth ring. "Hello?"

"Hi, Dr. Garriso. It's Cass. How's my favorite historian doing?" I asked.

"Excellent, my dear. Top notch. What can I do for you?"

"I was hoping you could tell us the location of a broch on Glencarrough land. To the east of the main compound."

I heard him shuffling around, no doubt getting up to consult his maps. "I can do that. Not a problem. I believe that land was surveyed in the 1930s. Someone would have marked it down."

"Thank you," I said.

"My pleasure. I'll send you the information by text when I find it."

"Perfect. Have a good one, Dr. Garriso."

"You as well."

The line disconnected, and I hit *End.* I was glad to hear Dr. Garriso sounding like himself again. It'd taken him some time to recover after his abduction last month, but it seemed like he was back to normal.

Nix stuck her head in the room. "You find something?"

"I think so. Dr. Garriso will let us know. Shouldn't take long. I think we're good to head over there. The drive will take a couple hours."

"Excellent. Let's get cracking, then. I'm ready to get to the bottom of this mystery."

So was I.

# CHAPTER THIRTEEN

I frowned down at the text message on my phone. "Dr. Garriso says that the broch isn't on the map."

Aidan looked over at me from the driver's side of his Range Rover. "But the land was surveyed."

"Yeah. And Dr. Garriso confirms it. They did the survey in 1931. There are a few archaeological sites on the map that were created then, but no brochs."

"That's weird," Nix said from the back seat.

She was piled in with Connor and Emile. Del and Claire sat in the fold-up seat in the very back.

"I trust Aethelred," Del said. "He said we'd have help finding it, so I say we give it a go and see what happens."

"Yeah." I wanted whatever answers Aethelred said were at the other end of this broch. "We'll just have to split up and look for it."

I shoved the phone back into my pocket and looked out the window at the sweeping vista of mountains. They rolled softly into the distance, covered in late summer heather. It was now mid-afternoon, and we were close to the Alpha Council stronghold. As we neared the eastern side of the compound, the road dipped down into a valley.

I kept my eye on the compass indicator that flashed blue from the rearview mirror. When it showed that we were directly east of Glencarrough, I said, "I think we should pull over here."

We were deep in the valley in a large section of woods. Aidan pulled the car over onto the side of the road, and we all piled out.

The light was dimmer here, cut off by the gnarled old trees on either side of the road.

"I'd say we're on the right track," Del said.

I glanced around at the forest, which had a distinctly ancient and creepy vibe.

"So, where is the help that Aethelred promised?" Emile asked.

Ralph and Rufus sat on each of his shoulders, their little noses twitching as they took in the woody scent of the forest.

"I have a feeling we have to look for it." I peered into the dark forest. Whatever kind of assistance we could expect, I didn't think it'd be hanging out by the roadside.

"Let's split up then and look in different directions," Aidan said. "We have a lot of ground to cover."

"Nix, Del, and I have comms charms," I said. "So we'll each go with a different group. We can call if we find something."

"Dibs on Emile and Ralph and Rufus!" Nix said, scratching Rufus's little head.

"Good." Del grinned. "I want Connor and Claire."

Though I had no memory of it myself, I'd seen kids pick their sports teams this way on TV.

"Then I'm with Aidan." I smiled at him. "We'll set off directly west. Del, how about your group goes northeast and Nix, yours goes southeast? You find anything, you contact the rest of us."

"On it." Del saluted, then winked at Connor and Claire.

We split up, Aidan and I cutting west through the woods. The land dipped down as we walked until soon we came to a wide river. The water was clear at the edges, burbling over round pebbles, but deep in the middle.

"This feeds Loch Tummel, I think," Aidan said. "If we follow it, it should take us roughly west."

As we walked along the river, my gaze constantly scanned the forest, taking in the gnarled trees and dappled sunlight spotting the ground. Animals rustled in the underbrush and a few squirrels chittered, but overall, it was weirdly quiet.

Splashing water sounded to my right, and I glanced over.

A head had popped out of the water in the middle of the river where it was so deep it was nearly black. The woman was beautiful, with flowing golden hair and strings of pearls wrapped around her neck. Weeds were woven through her hair, bright green and shiny, and they actually looked really good, considering the fact they were weeds.

"A Ceasg," Aidan said.

"Yeah." She had to be one of the highland mermaids, because I seriously doubted that a human would be out splashing in this river, her hair intricately decorated with weeds while she wore eighteen strands of her best pearls.

"Are you Cassiopeia McFane?" the Ceasg called.

I started at being called by my original, given name. I'd just learned it and hadn't taken to really using it yet. But how did she know it?

"Maybe?" I said.

"You are!" Her voice was delighted, and she swam closer, her tail flashing pink as she neared. I remembered that Ceasg were said to have the tails of salmon. I wondered briefly how she'd got her pearls if she wasn't an ocean mermaid. Perhaps she traded for them.

She splashed into the shallows, sitting upright on the pebbles. Up close, I noticed that her skin was slightly pink as well, glowing with a pearlescent sheen.

"About time you got here!" She splashed her tail. "I've been waiting ages."

"For me? Really?"

She nodded vigorously, her green eyes bright. I tried not to make eye contact, remembering advice about not meeting the gaze of a mermaid else they compelled you to follow them to their watery home. Or something like that.

"Of course," she said. "We've been waiting for you. *Finally* the time is here." Worry shadowed her gaze. "Though perhaps I shouldn't be so excited about that."

"What are you talking about? And who is *we?*"

"The Ceasg of Loch Tummel, of course. It has been our duty for centuries to guard this river and wait for The One."

*The One?* Oh, hell no. "What do you mean, the one?"

"The fated one who will save us from the darkness."

I was *so* not qualified to be The One.

"Explain," Aidan demanded. "With detail."

She sighed and flicked her hair back, flinging water droplets that plinked into the river. "Honestly, I'd expected you to be more knowledgeable about this whole thing. How else will you save us?"

"With your help?" I said.

She brightened at that. "Oh, I like that!"

"But you'll have to explain at the beginning."

"There's not much to say. The time has neared for the darkness to awaken. Our prophecy says so, and we can feel it in the energy of the water."

There seemed to be a lot of prophecies and fate lately. It made me nervous.

"The Ceasg do not want the darkness to rise," she said. "To keep that from happening, I'm supposed to direct you toward the broch and warn you about the demon on four legs. The Nuckelavee." She shuddered as she pointed away from the river toward a path that cut through the forest. "You must follow that path. Beware the Nuckelavee that seeks to intercept you. It is a creature of pure evil and would like the darkness to rise. You must escape it."

"How?"

"I don't know. There is no fresh water to cross in that direction. That is all that will stop the Devil of the Sea."

"The Devil of the Sea?" Aidan looked around. "Here?"

"He comes to land when he can," she said. Fear glinted in her eyes, and her skin turned sallow. "Beware him. Send him back to the sea if you can. But whatever you do, you must reach the broch."

That was all super mysterious. "Anything else?"

"You may trust the two-legged and the no-legged." She gestured to her pink fin. "But not the four-legged. Follow the path to your answers."

"This is all pretty cryptic," I said.

She frowned and nodded. "That's all I know, though. Prophecies don't exactly come with instructions. But good luck. We are relying on you."

I nodded and thanked her, then turned and set off for the path with Aidan. We were on an official quest now if a mermaid had given us instructions.

"That was weird," I said.

"I think it's going to get a lot weirder."

I called Del and Nix on their comms charms to tell them where we were and that we had a lead. They were miles away from us, but would head in this direction and hopefully catch up. Aidan and I walked quickly through the forest, our footsteps crunching on twigs and leaves. Magic vibrated in the air, dark and light at the same time.

As if good magic and dark magic filled the space, fighting for supremacy. This forest was alive with it. Something fueled this place, but I wasn't sure *what*.

Nervous sweat broke out on my skin as we walked and waited for the Nuckelavee.

"Maybe it won't show up," I muttered, thinking about how frightened the Ceasg had been.

"Maybe I'll—"

Something crashed in the distance, branches breaking and wood popping, cutting Aidan off. All animals and rustling silenced as the crashing grew louder.

I tensed, glancing around. For a moment, all I saw was the forest.

Then an enormous beast crashed through the trees—a horse the size of a Range Rover, ridden by a grotesque man with a wide, gaping mouth full of fangs. It was the most terrible thing I'd ever seen, straight from nightmares I couldn't have imagined.

Ice shivered down my spine. No, that man wasn't riding the horse. He was *part* of the horse, growing straight out of the horse's back. His arms hung down low, almost to the ground. Worse, the creature had no skin. Just shiny muscles and veins pulsing with black blood.

Shimmering gray light flashed around Aidan as he transformed into a griffin. His golden coat and feathers were a marked contrast to the Nuckelavee's slimy inside-out appearance, but his huge beak looked vicious.

Aidan launched himself at the Nuckelavee, his huge wings carrying him into the air. He dived, taking a chunk out of the demon-horse's side before the creature swiped at him with a long arm. The power in the punch sent Aidan flying through the air.

He crashed into a wide tree trunk and collapsed to the ground. As he rose unsteadily, I called upon my magic, letting the crackle and burn of lightning flow through my body. My heart pounded. When it had gathered enough, I released it, sending a cracking bolt toward the Nuckelavee.

Thunder boomed as it struck the creature in the chest. But instead of seizing and dropping, the Nuckelavee raised up on hind legs and whinnied ecstatically, glowing from within.

It was *feeding* on the lightning.

Of course. It was a creature from hell. Lightning and flame would only delight it. As my mind raced for a solution, Aidan charged the Nuckelavee again. The creature caught sight of him and turned to confront the attack.

They collided, a sickening clash of claws and teeth. The Nuckelavee tore at the griffin with his deadly claws while Aidan clamped his massive jaws around one of the creatures hind legs.

Aidan was as strong as the Nuckelavee, but they were both so vicious that his injuries would be dire if this continued.

*Think, think!*

The Ceasg had warned that there was no fresh water to cross to stop the devil of the sea. Water!

I called upon my power, mirroring Aidan's Elemental Mage powers. I rarely worked with water, but the cool, refreshing feel of it brushing against my skin told me I had the hang of it. I let the power surge in my chest as I envisioned a massive jet of water shooting from my hands.

Aidan and the Nuckelavee thrashed on the ground, tearing at each other, as I hit them with a massive stream of water. It felt cold and bright against my palms as it shot toward the Nuckelavee.

The demon creature howled as a deluge of water splashed against its hide. A massive cloud of steam burst up, obscuring the fight. The steam disappeared in time to show the soaking wet Nuckelavee right before the beast collapsed in a rush of water.

Griffin Aidan stood ankle deep in the puddle in the middle of the forest.

"Whew." I dragged a hand over my forehead. "I guess we've sent him back to the sea."

A swirl of gray light surrounded Aidan just before he returned to his human form. Blood poured from a wound in his arm, and he clutched his side.

My heart thudded heavily at the sight, and I raced to him.

"Are you all right?" I examined the deep cut on his forearm, then gently peeled up his shirt to reveal a deeper one on his abdomen.

Aidan collapsed heavily to his knees, and true panic pierced me. I dropped down beside him, gazing into his eyes. They were blurred with pain. I didn't understand. The cuts were deep, but not enough to slow him down.

When a trickle of blood appeared at the corner of his mouth, my skin turned ice cold.

*Internal bleeding.*

Of course. The Nuckelavee must have stomped on him with its great hooves.

Aidan fell onto his side. I cried out, too terrified for tears.

"Aidan!"

He gasped harshly but couldn't speak.

My heart pounded as fear crawled along my skin.

He was dying. Aidan was *dying.*

My hands shook as I tried to think of how to help him, but my terror slowed me. The golden cuff at my wrist caught my eye, and a thought pierced me.

I tugged off the cuff and threw it away. Magic swelled inside me, making me shake as a current ran through me. I reached for Aidan's healing powers, hoping to mirror them. They weren't strong—not enough to heal wounds as terrible as his—but I hoped that with my massive amount of power, I could enhance them enough to save him.

The idea of losing control made my breath catch in my throat. If I lost control trying to heal him, I'd kill him.

But his skin was so pale, his gaze now almost vacant.

I had to try.

My power grasped ahold of his. The forest scent of his magic was weaker than normal and I could barely hear the sound of crashing waves. But it was there. The healing gift was ephemeral, like a subtle smoke that I had to grasp onto.

I caught it and pulled it toward me, imagining mending all of Aidan's wounds. I ran my shaking hands gently over his body, forcing the healing energy into him.

My palms warmed, and the backs of my hands glowed red.

Tremors rocked my body as I knelt over Aidan. Tears that wouldn't fall burned at my eyes as I kept my gaze glued to his pale form. The magic inside me pulsed and surged, trying to break free. I shook with it, almost losing control.

I sucked in a deep breath and focused, pushing more healing energy into his body.

Slowly, the color returned to his skin. His gaze cleared. I glanced down at the wound on his arm, noting that the skin had knit itself back together.

"Cass," Aidan croaked.

My gaze jumped to his. Joy flared hot and bright inside me at the sight of his smile. All the color had returned to his face, and his eyes were clear.

"You're okay." Tears finally started to fall, now that the moment for action was gone. They poured down my face, hot and salty when they reached the corners of my mouth.

Aidan pushed himself upright and pulled me into his arms. I really started sobbing then, the reality of what had almost happened hitting me.

"It's okay," he murmured. "I'm fine. You healed me."

I clutched at him, running my hands over every inch I could reach to confirm that he really was okay.

"You almost died," I whispered.

"Yeah." He laughed. "But you saved me."

I pulled back, glaring at him. "You're laughing?"

He grinned. "You saved me, Cass. I was a breath away from dying, but I'm here. Because of you."

"So, you're laughing."

"It's amazing." His grin widened. "You're amazing."

I sat back on my heels, and a laugh bubbled out of me. Not because I thought I was amazing, but because I couldn't believe my good luck. And probably also because I was coming down from the adrenaline high of a lifetime.

"Laughing in the forest when you have things to be accomplishing? Tsk tsk." The creaky old voice sounded from the trees behind me.

I whirled on my knees, searching for the owner of the voice. A small figure walked out of the woods. He was no bigger than a child, with the legs of a goat and a wizened old man's face. A brown cloak was draped over his back.

"You may trust the two-legged and the no-legged," the Ceasg had said.

I really didn't want to hurt this little, uh, creature, so I hoped the Ceasg had been right.

"Who are you?" I asked, keeping my magic at the ready. Adrenaline was still coursing through my body, making me doubt my ability to maintain my control.

"I am MacKintosh, a Bauchan."

I'd heard of Buachans before. "Are you the helpful kind of hobgoblin or the tricky kind?"

He grinned, his teeth bright white. "Both. But in your case, I am here to help. I will lead you to the broch."

He gestured with an overly large hand, beckoning us to follow.

I glanced at Aidan.

He nodded. "I trust him."

It was enough for me. And after the stress of all that had just happened, I really didn't want to fight again.

As we climbed to our feet, I paid close attention to Aidan. My heartbeat calmed when I noticed how steady he was. I swooped down and grabbed my dampening cuff, shoved it on my wrist, then followed Aidan and MacKintosh.

"Lovely weather we're having, isn't it?" MacKintosh asked as he led us toward the broch.

"Yes," I said, following him off the path and into a more heavily forested part of the wood.

"I myself prefer a bit more rain, but I know how you lot prefer the sunshine," MacKintosh said.

He kept up a running stream of commentary as we walked through the forest. I kept one ear on his chatter and one ear out for trouble. The sun was setting, and the forest grew dark, leaving shadowed nooks that made for perfect hiding places.

I didn't get the impression that MacKintosh's chattiness was because he was particularly comfortable in this section of woods, but rather that he just liked to talk. He went a mile a minute, commenting on everything from the flora and fauna to the latest centaur football match that had lit up supernatural televisions last night.

He led us on such a circuitous route, in between trees and over gullies. I had no idea where we were by the time we reached a clearing in the woods. No wonder the surveyors hadn't found this place when they'd made their maps. My head was buzzing from trying to keep an eye out for danger while not offending our guide.

"And here it is." MacKintosh swept his arms out to indicate a stone tower in serious disrepair.

The sun had fully set, and the moon was behind clouds, so it was hard to make out the details of the tower. But the thing was huge—easily forty feet wide and half as tall. One whole side had tumbled down, revealing massively thick walls.

"Not very impressive now, but give it a moment," MacKintosh said.

I nodded, unsure of what he meant, and approached the broch slowly.

"Can we just walk in?" I asked, hoping there weren't enchantments we had to get around.

"Wait until the moon shines upon it," he said.

I glanced up, noticing that the moon was about to break free of some clouds, which glowed white at the edges. When the moon finally peaked out, I glanced back at the broch.

I stutter-stepped, surprised to see that the broch was now twice as tall and the wall had been repaired. There was even a conical wooden roof on top.

"What happened?" Aidan asked from beside me.

"Beats me." I studied the broch, which would have been an excellent defensive structure in the Iron Age. I was about to call Nix and Del on my comms charm to tell them we'd found it when MacKintosh's voice sounded behind us.

"Quick! The moon will disappear soon. You can only enter in the moonlight, so go now!"

I glanced back at him to see him shooing us, his brown gaze bright in the moonlight. "I need to tell my friends we've found it."

"No time! Go, go!"

The panic in his gaze convinced me. I turned back to the broch and approached, entering a darkened archway. A heavy wooden door was positioned inside, but it was propped open. As I stepped through, I caught a glimpse of movement inside the broch.

But when Aidan and I entered fully, everything was dark and empty. The walls were once again broken, and the roof was gone.

"Moon's gone back behind the clouds," Aidan said.

"Yeah." I shivered. The enchantment was eerie, flashing this place in and out of existence at the whim of the moon.

We explored the interior of the broch for a moment, but there was nothing inside. Just a few dark gaps in the thick walls. I was about to explore one when the world lit up with sound and noise.

It took me a moment to realize.

"The moon has come out from behind clouds," I murmured. The walls were once again complete, but it was the hustle and bustle inside the broch that was so unexpected.

A fire glowed in the middle while people sat and stood all over the small space. They were semi-transparent, as was the fire, but they were living their lives like it was a normal day. Someone was cooking, and another was weaving. Several men sat on benches around the hearth, chatting.

I glanced up, and the sight of the platforms extending out from the walls above made my head spin. There were multiple stories in the broch, but the center column was open all the way to the roof to allow the fire's smoke to escape. There were people on the upper levels, too, though I couldn't tell what they were doing.

But no one seemed to notice us.

"We're invisible to them," Aidan said.

"Yeah." I realized that I couldn't quite make out what everyone was saying. Not because they spoke an old version of Scots dialect that I didn't understand, but because their voices were muted in the same way that their figures were. Like they were half on this plane and half in the next.

"I suppose we should look around," he said. "The entrance is supposed to be in here somewhere."

"I want to check out that gap in the wall there," I said.

Aidan nodded. We cut through the broch, dodging people and two small piglets as we made our way to the gap in the wall. When we reached it, we had to wait for a woman to move out of the way.

Eventually, she did, going into the gap in the wall and turning left. I followed her, watching her climb up narrow stone steps sandwiched between the thick exterior walls of the broch. When she disappeared at the top, having gone out onto one of the wooden platforms, I looked right.

There was a set of stairs leading down, into the ground.

"Those look promising," Aidan said.

I nodded and stepped toward the stairs. As soon as my foot landed on the top stair, the magic hit me, rolling over me in waves. My dragon covetousness welled, the strongest I'd ever felt.

"Very promising," I gasped. "There's something really valuable down here. I feel it."

Slowly, I made my way down the narrow stairs, using the walls for support. Aidan followed close behind. I shook my right hand, igniting the lightstone ring so that the yellow glow filled the dark spaces.

The stairs went on forever.

"Thank magic I'm not claustrophobic," I said. Still, my heart raced.

At the bottom, a passageway carved out of the earth led into the darkness.

"Super creepy," I said. But my dragon sense roared. Whatever was at the end of the tunnel, I wanted it. *Bad.*

"Watch out for traps," Aidan said as we started down the tunnel.

"Will do." This looked like just the type of place to have them.

But as I walked, I felt nothing but welcome. Like I was supposed to be here.

*This was all fated.* From Aethelred's prophecy to the Ceasg, Nuckelavee, and MacKintosh who waited for me. This place that welcomed me was just icing on the cake.

It terrified me. Not just because I wasn't sure I could accomplish whatever I was fated to do, but because

Aethelred had prophesied one of our deaths. Me, Nix, or Del. It was the thought of losing Del or Nix that scared me most. It was crazy, but I hoped it was me. I'd meant it when I'd said I didn't want to live in a world without them.

"You've been pretty silent up there." Aidan's voice snapped me out of my dark thoughts.

"Yeah, uh, sorry. Just focusing." Why was I lying to him? He loved me. Besides Nix and Del, he'd been my biggest supporter ever. "Actually, I'm just really worried about all this. And Nix and Del."

Aidan's big hand gripped my shoulder comfortingly. "It will be okay."

I relaxed a little, wanting to believe him. But I kept my wariness wrapped around myself like a cloak as I walked through the passageway. No booby-traps appeared, though. The feeling of belonging remained, as well as the sense that there was a massive amount of treasure at the end of this passage.

"If I find Smaug crouched on a pile of gold at the end of this tunnel, I won't be a bit surprised," I said.

Aidan chuckled, and we kept going, occasionally having to duck beneath a tree root or dodge around a boulder protruding from the dirt walls.

"We've gone at least four miles," Aidan said after almost an hour.

"We must be near Glencarrough, then."

Ten minutes later, my dragon sense roared so strong within me that my palms started sweating and my heart pounded.

"We're *so close*." It was hard to get the words out. My whole body was vibrating with the sense that we were near the greatest treasure I'd even encountered.

When the tunnel spilled into a massive cavern, I had to blink to make out what was within. A pedestal sat in the middle of the space. A bright golden glow shined from it, nearly blinding me.

But I didn't need sight to find it. My dragon sense pulled me toward it, and I followed it without hesitation. I just wanted to touch whatever made that glow. To hold it in my hands.

"Stop!" A sharp voice cracked in the silence.

I stumbled to a halt, though I wanted to race to the pedestal. But the voice commanded attention, and I gave it. Aidan and I waited silently for a figure to join the voice.

The air was so stale that I wondered how much oxygen was actually in the room. This place was long abandoned.

The figure that approached from the side of the cavern was nearly transparent. She glowed with the same golden light that emitted from the pedestal, though she was paler. When she neared, I realized that her face was featureless. As if someone had just erased whatever had been there and left a blank slate. I wasn't sure why I thought she was a woman, though I was certain of it.

"You are Cassiopeia McFane," she said as she neared.

"I am. Who are you?"

"The Watcher of the Power."

"That's quite a title." She didn't laugh at my lame joke. I fidgeted. "What is this place?"

"Come." She led me over to the pedestal.

As we neared, I realized that an egg sat upon it, large and black and shot through with golden veins of light. It seemed to vibrate.

But it wasn't the sight that hit me so hard in the chest. It was the power. It was dark and light, Shifter and Magica. It was everything. Life, death, joy, sadness. A blank slate of magic and power that could fuel the world.

Did it?

"What is this?" I asked. It had to be what Victor wanted, but what exactly *was* it?

"It is the Stone of Power." She held her hand out to it, but didn't touch. "It is the reason that Glencarrough was built here."

"Is it evil or good?" I asked, trying to get a feel for it. My fingertips itched to touch it, but I dared not.

"Either. The evil one seeks to break it open and make the power his own. If he does, it will become evil. And he'll be capable of the greatest magic the world has ever known."

I swallowed hard. That was really bad.

"The Heartstone and Glencarrough protect not only their stronghold, but this as well," she said. "For thousands of years, it has been protected by those who live here. You walked through one such community when you entered."

"The broch was built there to protect this?"

"Yes. It is one of the most important magical artifacts ever found. No one knows where it comes from, but it contains more magical energy than any thing or person in the world." Her head turned toward me. "Even you."

I clenched my fist to keep from touching it. "Is it a dragon egg?"

"Perhaps. If so, it would make sense that you are the one prophesied to protect it."

It did make sense, though that was a lot of responsibility. "Can I just take it and hide it somewhere else?"

"No. Only great magic can remove it from here. You do not possess that. Not alone."

"Not alone?"

"You would need your companions to do that— Death and Life. With them, you can remove the stone."

Okay. So I just had to come back here with Nix and Del, and we'd take this thing and hide it somewhere else.

"Why us and not the Alpha Council? Don't they live here to protect it?"

"Yes. And for many centuries they have. They are the descendants of the people in the broch. But what is coming is stronger than they are. Only the Triumvirate can defeat it."

*Oh, man.* The words put a thousand-pound weight on my shoulders.

"To protect the Stone of Power, you must defeat the one who seeks to use it for his ill will," she said.

*Victor.* "Any tips on how to do that?"

She nodded. She had no features, so I couldn't tell if she smiled, but I thought she might. "You can only defeat him away from his Circle of Power. On familiar ground where you can draw from ancient power that is yours."

"What the hell does that mean, exactly?"

"I do not know. I am not a seer. That is part of the message I was meant to pass to you, but it is all I know."

Excellent. Super cryptic advice that was vital to my success. My favorite kind. "Is there another part of the message?"

"Yes. You must embrace your magic to succeed."

"How? I've tried."

Her head nodded toward the cuff. "You must remove your crutch and have faith in yourself."

I held up my wrist. "This protects my friends."

"You don't need it. When you embraced your magic to save Aidan, you were successful. Forgo the crutch and believe in yourself."

"Okay." It scared the hell out of me, but I'd do it. I'd been relying on this thing too long.

"You must go now, Cassiopeia McFane. The time is drawing near."

"There's nothing else you want to tell me?" Anything? Step-by-step instructions? A map? Because I really felt like I could use some help with this.

She shook her head. "No. Now go. And do not fail."

# CHAPTER FOURTEEN

It took Aidan and me a full two hours to make our way out of the tunnel and back across the forest. MacKintosh had been waiting for us when we'd departed the broch, and he'd led us back to the river where we'd met the Ceasg. She'd been gone and the river silent, no doubt pleased that her job was done.

We met everyone back at the car. They'd found nothing. We were dirty and tired as we piled into the seats. As soon as I sat down, I took off the dampening cuff that I'd been wearing and put it in the cup holder, letting the magic flow through me. I was going to follow the Watcher's advice to the T, and honestly, it felt good to get rid of the dampening charm.

While Aidan drove us back toward his land, I told everyone what we'd learned.

"So, do we go to the Alpha Council with this information, or do we try to move the stone ourselves?" Nix asked.

"I don't know where we'd put it if we moved it ourselves," Del said.

I agreed with her. What had seemed easy in the cavern—take the stone and move it—now seemed a lot more complex. Where could we store it? If that crazy underground cavern wasn't safe, then what was?

Aidan turned the Range Rover off the main road and onto the gravel drive that led to his land. My mind was so heavy with exhaustion and worry that I almost didn't notice the prickle of the oncoming protection charms that guarded his property.

Before we could cross over the line onto his land, noise and light exploded around us. A massive force hit the car, flipping it into the air. It crashed to the ground, roof first. Metal screamed and crunched. A dull noise blared in my head as I hung suspended upside down, strapped to my seat by the seatbelt.

All around me, the world was chaos. Smoke rolled across the ground outside. Flames licked at the hood of the car. My friends were struggling in their seats.

"Run!" I gasped.

I grabbed my dagger at my thigh and sawed frantically at my seatbelt. It broke apart, and I crashed onto the roof of the car in a heap. Beside me, Aidan was free and climbing out through the broken glass window. In the back seat, my friends were scrambling out as well.

Aidan reached for me. "Come on, Cass!"

My window hadn't broken, so I started for him, glass cutting my palms. But the window behind me shattered and something grabbed my legs, pulling me out. I shrieked and twisted around to see what had gotten ahold of me.

A shadow demon was gripping my calves. I threw out my hand and blasted him with magic, not even stopping to think of what I was throwing. A spear of ice flew from my hand and struck him in the chest, throwing him back.

On the other side of the car, a shadow demon gripped an unconscious Nix around her waist. A millisecond later, he stepped into a silvery black cloud and disappeared.

On the other side of the car, Emile stood, dumbstruck. Next to him, the familiar gray light surrounded Aidan as he transformed into a griffin, ready to attack. I whirled around to find more demons to kill, but something hard hit me on the back of the head. Pain pierced my skull, blinding me.

Darkness followed.

Cold stone pressed against my cheek, and every muscle in my body ached. Something scratchy bound by wrists behind my back. My ankles were tied, too. Worse, I felt the familiar deadening sensation of the Gundestrop cauldron.

My skin chilled as my heart began to thud. I worked at the bindings on my wrists, trying to wiggle free as I cracked open dry eyes and saw an expanse of cobblestone ground stretched out before me. It glowed gray in the dim light of the moon.

Pain streaked through my skull as I looked up, rolling my eyeballs because I could hardly turn my head. Clouds drifted in front of the moon, glowing white at the edges. A strange blue light streaked through the sky like a starburst, but I couldn't see where it came from. I kept working at the bindings around my wrists, but they didn't give an inch.

"Cass?" Del whispered from behind me.

My head pounded as I rolled to see her. She lay tied on the ground behind me, with Nix on the other side of her. We were all bound and tossed on the ground like garbage. Where were our friends? Fates, I hoped they'd made it out of that ambush all right.

I looked behind Del. My stomach lurched. There were demons, all standing with their backs toward us. Dozens of them, maybe a hundred.

"They're surrounding us," Del said.

"Yeah," I croaked. I looked beyond them, searching for Victor. There were walls circling the cobblestones we lay upon. They looked familiar. "We're in the courtyard at Glencarrough."

Figures stood at the tops of the walls. The Shifter guards. But they were frozen solid, some with their weapons raised, others in mid-shout. All were in human form. A ray of blue light pierced each. My eyes traveled along one of the rays, finally finding its termination point at a brilliant blue gem that hung suspended in the air.

The Heartstone. Somehow, Victor had turned its magic against the Shifters. It had frozen them solid.

But where was he? My bindings weren't giving way, and fear raced through my veins like acid.

A sound echoed from the other side of the courtyard, like metal against stone. I rolled and looked over, seeing Dermot and Victor about twenty feet away.

"Ah, awake, are we?" Victor's cold voice echoed across the courtyard.

Dermot stood at his side, a pathetic lackey. Behind him, Elenora was frozen on the steps of the main building. More Shifters were frozen around her, as if they'd heard a disturbance and come running.

Except Victor had frozen them all.

The Gundestrop cauldron sat on the stone ground in front of Dermot, right in the middle of the courtyard. Victor clutched the Chalice of Youth in his hand. It glimmered dully in the light of the moon, but the sight of all three artifacts made me swallow hard.

Victor had everything he needed, including us. He approached, his steps measured. But his eyes gleamed dark, avarice and evil so easy to see.

"The time has finally come, my dears." He slipped a hand into his pocket and withdrew a knife. His gaze drifted from mine and landed on Nix. "I think I will start with you."

Del and I thrashed, struggling up and lunging for him. A big hand grabbed me and threw me back. I caught a glimpse of a shadow demon just before his boot came down on my stomach, pinning me in place.

Another pinned Del, though Nix was still unconscious. A shadow demon stood at her side, ready to step on her if she woke.

Though the cauldron's dampening charm suppressed most of my magic, I still had access to a little bit of it.

But with my hands tied behind my back, I couldn't shoot lightning at my enemy. I didn't have enough power to create a big enough illusion to fool them.

Could I shift and get out of my bindings that way? With my hands free, I'd at least have some of my lightning. I closed my eyes and focused on the embers of my magic, trying to fan them into flame. Images of turning into a wolf flashed in my mind.

Shifting had always been one of the harder gifts for me to master, but I'd managed in the past. I tried to force the magic through my veins, willing the familiar warmth to fill my limbs as I changed shape.

But nothing happened. My limbs stayed cold, and my form stayed human.

*Damn it!* What good was infinite power if I couldn't use it?

Victor crouched next to Nix, setting the cup at her side.

"Stop it!" I shrieked, knowing it would do no good.

The demon's boot pressed harder on my stomach, shutting me up. I tried the last thing I could think of, reaching out for Del's magic. If I could mirror it, I could transport us out of here.

My power reached out for hers, seeking the clean laundry smell and the gift of transporting.

I came up cold. The cauldron dampened her gift, so there was nothing there for me to mirror. I'd been able to mirror the guards' magic in the Prison for Magical Miscreants because they'd worn the cuffs that made their power active.

I tried not to let hopelessness take over. There was a way out of this. There had to be.

I looked over at Nix and Victor, who knelt at her side. She was still unconscious, her brown hair spread across the cobblestone.

A creepy smile tugged at the corner of Victor's mouth as he turned Nix's head and dragged the dagger across the side of her throat.

"Stop it!" I shrieked.

Nix jerked upright, her eyes flaring wide. The cut wasn't deadly, though it bled freely. The demon at her side gripped her shoulders, holding her still.

"What the hell!" she shouted.

She kicked, but Victor dodged her legs, pressing the goblet to the side of her throat and letting the blood pour into it.

The golden chalice began to smoke and glow bright.

"The chalice's immortality is enhancing her blood," Victor said.

"Stop it, you bastard!" Nix yelled.

Victor removed the goblet and stood, then walked over to the cauldron and poured the blood into it. The silver vessel glowed an eerie red, the decorative impressions highlighted ghoulishly. He shook out the last of the blood, then approached us again.

"What the hell is your problem, Victor?" I demanded. My heart pounded a fierce staccato in my chest.

"Oh, I'm sure you can imagine," he said as he crouched by Del.

She spat at him, and he smacked her, then grabbed her hair and cut her neck with his blade. She shrieked and kicked, but her wound wasn't deadly either. Just enough to fill the goblet with blood.

I'd been wrong about Victor. He hadn't wanted my power. Or at least, he no longer wanted it. After he'd failed to steal it from me as a child, he'd set his sights on a bigger prize.

But he still needed me to get it. The Watcher of the Power had said that only the Triumvirate could move the Stone of Power. Apparently, our blood could do that just fine. Especially if it was "enhanced" by the Chalice of Youth.

I thrashed against the demon's hold above me. Until my hands were unbound or I could at least roll over to shoot them with lightning, my power was useless. But the demon pressed his boot harder into my stomach, not letting me move an inch.

Victor knelt at my side, and bile rose in my throat. I could hear Del and Nix screaming at him, but my rage drowned out their exact words.

"You bastard," I hissed. "You cowardly, miserable piece of shit. Using your parents' deaths as an excuse to be a fucking asshole. You're weak."

That last one got to him. His impassive brown gaze flared slightly, and he smacked me across the face. Pain flared in my cheek as my head whipped sideways. Head still spinning, I felt the knife cut into my neck.

I thrashed and struggled as the demon held me still. The wound burned as my blood flowed into the cup. I could hear it sizzle when it hit the golden goblet.

Miserable as it was, the process was over too soon. He was that much closer to his goal. Victor stood and walked away from me, the goblet clutched in his hand.

"Is that it?" Del screamed. "That's all you've got? Taking our blood and pouring it in your stupid cauldron?"

"Hardly," Victor said.

I thrashed against my bindings and the demon who pinned me. I'd rubbed my wrists raw and the rope slid against blood, but it wasn't enough to allow my wrists to slip free.

I kept my gaze on Victor and Dermot, who watched his master avidly. *Fucking moron.* Victor wasn't going to share the power with him. He'd be lucky if Victor didn't sacrifice him as part of this sick ritual.

Victor poured the goblet of my blood into the cauldron. The silver glowed an even brighter red as it flowed in. When the goblet was empty, Victor tossed it in too. The whole thing flared red and silver. Victor raised his hands over the top, and an inky black fluid flowed from his fingertips into the cauldron. The scent of rot and decay rolled toward me. I gagged.

His magic. He was somehow pouring his magic into the cauldron with our blood.

The potion within began to smoke and bubble, flowing up over the top. What was he going to do with it?

Panic and fear drowned out rational thought.

We were failing! We were fated to fix this, and we were failing! Hundreds of Shifters would die when he got all the power he sought. More, probably. *Us.*

Victor stepped back from the cauldron, which glowed a brilliant red and smoked like Vesuvius. A second later, the whole thing melted, collapsing in a pile of melted silver and vile potion.

What the hell?

It flowed in one direction, a glowing orange river that began to form the shape of a star.

The emblem in the middle of the courtyard! I noticed it the last time I was here, when I'd been knocked out of the sky by the Shifter's nets, but hadn't realized it was anything more than decoration.

But the cauldron was gone. As the potion filled in the crevices forming the shape of a star, I tried reaching for my magic to see if I could access it.

I got nothing but the usual trickle. Though the cauldron was gone, the melted metal was still imbued with the dampening charm. The silver was quickly cooling, turning from red to black. And the charm was still in effect. Now, it'd become part of the courtyard.

The potion still glowed red in the outline of the star. The earth began to tremble and Victor laughed, a victorious sound that made my skin chill. A great cracking noise rent the night as the ground split open where the potion soaked into the cobblestones. I jerked, trying to scramble back, but the demon held me fast.

The crack streaked open, ten feet long and at least three feet wide. A golden light shot up from the crevice, shooting into the night sky.

"No!" I cried. We must be right over the cavern that held the Stone of Power.

Victor approached the beam of light and held his hand into it. When his skin made contact, the light turned dark. Smoky. My heart thundered in my head. He was taking the neutral power and turning it evil! Taking it into himself.

A black cloud spread out from the vertical beam of light, slowly moving toward the ground to form a dome over us. It reeked of evil, making me shudder and gag.

Panic surged in my chest as I fought the demon who pinned me. We couldn't just lie here helplessly!

Above me, a flash of red and blue caught my eye. My gaze darted toward it. The dragonets! The four of them zoomed downward from high in the sky, coming to our rescue.

*We might make it out of this.*

Suddenly, more figures appeared in the courtyard. Aidan, Claire, Conner, and Emile. Some had bandages wrapped around limbs, but they were here. All alive. Somehow, they'd escaped Victor's ambush.

Then the League of FireSouls appeared. All nine of them. And finally, Aerdeca and Mordaca, dressed in their usual black and white. But it was combat gear this time.

Not only had my friends escaped, but they'd called for help and gotten transport charms from somewhere. Likely from the League of FireSouls, who'd had a stockpile last I'd seen them. They'd managed to break through Glencarrough's defenses because Victor had taken the Heartstone.

*Take that, you bastard.*

Hope flared bright even as the demons who'd surrounded us surged into the circle. At least two dozen made it inside before the smoky black dome slammed down around us. My friends were all trapped inside, but the numbers weren't terribly uneven.

Connor hurled a potion bomb at the glittering blue Heartstone that hovered in the air. It exploded against the stone in a cloud of green, knocking the thing to the ground. It clattered against the cobblestones, and the blue rays of light that had frozen the Shifters faded.

I could barely see through the hazy black dome that surrounded us, but I could make out movement on the top wall. Oh, thank magic, they were unfrozen.

They were still outnumbered by the demons, but at least they had a chance. At least *we* had a chance, with the shifters on our side. Battle exploded around me, fought hand to hand, weapon to weapon. No magic and no Shifting because of the cauldron.

Aidan charged the demon who pinned me, slamming into him and throwing him to the ground. I struggled to my feet just as Claire reached me. She slashed through my bindings with her sword, then raced to Del.

I spun toward Victor, ready to blast him with my lightning. I might not be at full power, but I was the only one with magic and I'd blast him until he fried. The golden light was continuing to flow into him, probably draining from the stone deep in the cavern below.

Behind Victor, Mordaca stood, her black hair whipping in the wind. She drew a black bow from her back and fired an arrow straight at him, her gaze deadly.

I wanted the kill for myself, but watching the projectile shoot toward his heart made joy leap in my own. He wasn't even looking.

But the arrow bounced off of him. Mordaca shrieked, then fired another. It bounced off as well. Finally, Victor glanced toward her, annoyed.

Would he attack or continue to absorb the power? I didn't want to find out. The battle raged around me as I called upon my magic, focusing on my gift of lightning. It crackled and burned beneath my skin, and I let it go, shooting it toward Victor.

Thunder cracked as the bolt bounced off of him, striking a nearby demon.

*Damn it!*

"How is he impervious?" Del yelled from where she fought a demon with her sword.

The Watcher's words came back to me. "He can't be hurt within his circle of power. *This* is his circle of power."

Nearby, Aidan fought off two demons. Aerdeca battled another, wielding a slender black sword like a pro. It was a war zone in here, people falling left and right. Blood everywhere.

"We have to get him out of here, then. Before he finishes his ritual," Nix yelled.

"On it!" Aidan yelled back. He charged Victor, slamming into him with all his might, clearly attempting to carry him outside of the smoky barrier.

Normally, he'd have no problem. But Victor didn't budge, fixed in place by the same magic that protected him from Mordaca's arrows and my lightning. Instead, he lashed out with an arm, throwing Aidan off him. Aidan flew twenty feet through the air, propelled by Victor's unnatural strength, and crashed into the ground.

Connor raced to him, fighting off a demon as Aidan rose.

Dread filled my chest, a black tar that made it hard to breath. I turned to Nix and Del, whose faces looked as panicked as I felt. The battle raged around us.

"What do we do?" I asked.

"I don't know!" Nix cried.

A flash of blonde hair caught my eye as a person shouted. Corin, the FireSoul leader.

"Corin!" I yelled. "Are there any more transport charms."

"No!" She yelled as she stabbed a demon through the stomach. "We used the last one to get here."

My head began to buzz as the terrible dread grew. No charms and my magic didn't hurt him. He was impervious to all attack.

"What do we do?" Nix cried.

"I know." Del's voice was deadly calm. "Cass will take my gift. She's the only one with the power to actually use it inside this hell bubble."

My heart dropped to my feet. "What do you mean, take your gift?"

Del's eyes were serious. "You know what I mean. You take my gift, like a FireSoul would. Then you can transport him out of here and kill him."

Bile rose in my throat as Nix gasped. "No! No, Del! She can just Mirror it."

My whole body turned to ice.

Del's voice was steady as she said, "No, she can't. She already tried when we were tied up. Right, Cass?"

"I tried." My voice was lead. Around us, the battle raged. Bodies were on the ground. Some of them had to be my friends. We were running out of time. "It didn't work."

Everything inside me screamed as Del said, "You have to do it, Cass. You heard the prophecy. One of us will fall, only to rise again. That's me."

Tears burned my eyes, and a rock lodged in my throat. "No," I croaked.

"I'm the one!" Del cried. "I am Death. What can dying do to me? I am the only one with a gift that can help you kill Victor. You must take it and defeat him."

"No!" I screamed. I couldn't think clearly. I didn't care if she was right. I didn't care about prophecy. All I could think about was losing Del. My world was pain and terror. "No!"

Del stepped forward. "I love you, Cass."

"No, Del—"

She thrust her sword through her chest. The silver blade sank deep, somewhere left of her heart.

Nix screamed. I might have screamed. I didn't know. There was a roaring in my head as I stared at Del.

She fell to her knees, her eyes wide. Blood marred her lips as she croaked, "Do it before...too late."

I dropped down beside her, tears blinding me. I clutched at her jacket, sobbing. "Del, no! Del!"

Her eyes met mine, pleading.

Steal her power? I was supposed to steal *Del's* power? My *deirfiúr*?

Nix fell to her knees beside me and grabbed my shirt, shaking me. I looked up.

"Do it!" Her gaze was hard. "Now! If we don't defeat Victor, we won't be able to get her back!"

I sucked in a shuddery breath, my mind whirling with panic. Nix was right.

My heart skittered deep down in my chest like a frightened animal, unable to be present for what I was about to do. Pain such as I'd never felt surged through me as I looked down at Del, whose eyes were closing.

No. I couldn't be too late.

"I love you, Del." I sobbed as I pressed my hands to her chest and reached for her power. My stomach heaved as white flame licked down my arms and into Del.

No matter how long I lived or what I witnessed, this would be the worst moment of my life.

I forced myself to grasp hold of her transport gift. It was ephemeral and light, like a piece of gauze, but I grasped it and drew it into me.

When I'd taken the last of it, Del shuddered and lay still. I fell back, away from her body, and retched until there was nothing left in me.

My mind screamed at the horror of what I'd just done, but I shoved it aside.

Del was dead. There was no way in hell I'd fall apart and make her sacrifice worthless.

My mind was blank as I stumbled to my feet, unable to look at her for fear I'd fall apart again. I charged Victor. The battle raged on as I ran. I had one task, and I had to complete it. But where would I take him?

The Watcher's words drifted through my mind.

I could only defeat him on familiar ground, where I could draw from ancient power that was mine.

The Black Fort.

I was almost to Victor, who still stood above the crack in the ground, soaking up the magic. I hurled myself at him and hung on tight, reaching for my magic and Del's gift.

*Please, let me have enough.*

I envisioned the Black Fort and sent us through the ether, tearing Victor away from his horrible ritual and the devastation he had wrought.

# CHAPTER FIFTEEN

We crashed to the wet grass inside the Black Fort as pouring rain pounded down upon us. Victor's enraged roar was as loud as the thunder cracking in the distance. Away from the Gundestrop cauldron, the power that flowed through my veins was strong enough to take my breath. Like an electric current.

I tore at Victor's pockets, trying to make sure he had no transport charms. I wouldn't let him escape. Victor threw me off him and surged to his feet. His face was twisted with a rage unlike any I had ever seen.

As I scrambled up, I reached for my magic, but he hit me with a sonic boom that blasted me backward. I flew through the air and skidded on the wet grass. Raggedly, I sucked in air, my whole body aching like a giant had stepped on me.

*Shit, shit, shit.*

Weakly, I crawled behind a nearby standing stone. Victor stood in the center of the circle, not far from the statues of Del, Nix, and me.

"You can't hide, you worthless bitch," he roared.

Hide? As if I would hide.

I was supposed to call upon the power that was here and mine, according to the Watcher. But *how*?

I had no idea, but I needed to do something.

Rain poured down on me as I called upon my magic, gasping when it surged through me like a tidal wave. I'd make a lightning bolt so powerful it'd turn him to ash. As it cracked and burned beneath my skin, I envisioned a bolt the size of a train. I liked the idea of killing him with Aaron's gift. It would be a bit of vengeance for Victor's former slave.

When it had grown to full size and strength within me, I lunged from behind the stone and hurled it at him. The crack of thunder deafened me, and the blast of light blurred out our surroundings.

Just as the bolt was about to crash into Victor, he threw up a shield, deflecting it. It ricocheted off, crashing into a nearby standing stone. The rock exploded, sending shards straight for me.

I dodged, throwing myself to the ground and covering my head. When I looked up a second later, I saw Victor throwing another sonic boom at me. I tried to dodge, but it picked me up and threw me again.

When I crashed down, I tasted blood in my mouth.

I didn't stand a chance as long as he could see me. And I wasn't using my magic most effectively. Rage and pain made it hard to focus, but I tried to shove them aside, focusing only on killing Victor. I was fated to stop him. If I failed, then what? He'd finish the horrible job he started.

No way I could let that happen.

I lay still, playing dead as my magic prickled beneath my skin, ready to be released. I started with illusion, grasping the elusive filaments of the gift and imagining my body disappearing. The magic felt almost weightless as it flowed through me, making my limbs feel light. They disappeared, then my torso too. Victor's roar of rage indicated that my head had probably gone as well. I crawled away from where I'd lain so that he couldn't blast me.

But this wasn't good enough. I needed a distraction. I envisioned dozens of me, all running around inside the circle.

The first one appeared. Victor shot it with a sonic boom. The noise cracked in the air, making my eardrums ache, but the illusion of me was unaffected.

More illusions appeared until two dozen images of me ducked and weaved through the standing stones. Victor shot each one, roaring when the sonic booms did nothing.

Eventually, he'd hit the real me on a streak of luck. I had to act.

He was definitely trapped here without a transport charm and getting madder every second. He'd planned this for years, and I'd stopped him.

When his back was turned, I called upon my gift of lightning, sending a massive bolt right at his back. There was no way he'd turn in time to see it and block it.

He didn't block it. The bolt, which was as wide as he was tall, slammed right into his back. He flew forward onto his front. I expected to see him smoking and dead, a black crisp of a man.

Instead, he leapt to his feet, his rage palpable on the air. It seeped from him like a black fog.

"I'm done playing!" he roared.

The black fog that seeped from him grew thicker, swirling around him. His skin turned an ashen gray and bulged, rippling with some unseen force.

*What the hell?*

His body began to grow, upward and outward. The gray fabric of his suit ripped and tore. His skin was fully gray now, turning to black. It cracked in places, revealing a bright red glow, like lava under the surface of rock. It took only seconds, but soon he was twenty feet tall and had turned entirely to stone.

My stomach dropped to my feet. He was made of *stone*. How could I kill stone? Was this the new gift he'd taken from the Stone of Power? It must be. What would he be if he'd gotten all the stone's power?

He lumbered toward me, steam rising from the surface of his body as the rain hit the lava that seeped from between the cracks of rock.

My heart thundered so loud I swore he could probably hear it. Could he see me? A quick glance at my arms told me no. I was still invisible.

But he was upon me now, drawn by the sound of my heartbeat or some other kind of magic. I built up my lightning to hurl it at him, but his massive fist was too fast. It slammed into me, so big his hand made contact with my body from my legs to my head.

Blinding pain exploded through every inch of me.

I flew through the air, crashing into one of the statues. When I crumbled to the ground, I'd lost control of my illusion. I was visible again and could see my limbs, which looked twisted at odd angles. Breathing felt like being stabbed in the lungs with a million knives. I tried to sit, but I couldn't. My whole body was pain. Broken, dozens of bones snapped. Multiple ribs piercing my lungs.

On the other side of the stone circle, Victor smashed the upright standing stones. He was entirely absorbed in his rage.

Pain seared through me. I couldn't move. Not an inch.

Was this all over? Was I too broken to fight? Too destroyed to use my magic? What did I have that could defeat a man-made rock? There was probably a core of life in him somewhere, but I didn't know how to extinguish it.

But I had to think of a way. For my parents, who Victor had killed. For Del, who'd sacrificed herself so that I could do this.

Unable to sit, I gazed up at the statue. It was the one representing magic. Representing me. I could just make out the statues of Del and Nix—Life and Death.

The Watcher's words flashed in my mind. "A place from which you can draw power."

The statues.

When we'd been here last, Del and Nix had said they could feel their magic in the statues. Life and Death.

I needed both of those, and I was a Mirror Mage, wasn't I? Normally, mirroring the magic in a statue would be impossible. But nothing was normal here. *I* wasn't normal. Not anymore. My body might be broken, but my magic wasn't.

And Nix and Del would help me, even though they weren't here.

As Victor crushed the last of the standing stones on the other side of the circle, I reached out with my magic, stretching for the life in Nix's statue. I needed just a bit—enough to heal myself so I'd live long enough to deploy Del's gift.

When I grasped hold of the bright light of it, I nearly wept with relief as it flowed through me. My pain started to fade as Nix's life-giving force poured into me.

When I had enough that I thought I could stand, I cut the connection. But I wasn't stupid enough to get up and attract Victor's attention. He was consumed with rage, stomping toward me, swatting at standing stones as he came.

But he was made of rock, and he was slow. I might have just enough time...

I reached out for the magic in Del's statue, gasping when the cold touch of death flowed toward me. I couldn't hold on to this magic—it would kill me. Only Del could really do that.

I had to shoot it at Victor, and fast.

I flung my hands out, directing a stream of Del's deadly magic at Victor. It shot like a black bolt of lightning. Beneath it, the wet grass shriveled and died. When it slammed into Victor's stone chest, he stopped dead in his tracks.

I couldn't make out any expression on his stone face, but I imagined there was shock. The lava between his cracks of stone began to turn black, then crumbled to dust. It fell to the dead grass below his feet, a raining shower of disintegrated lava rock.

As the stones fell to the ground, one by one, I imagined Del in her last moments. My sister, my *deirfiúr*. Now, her power destroyed Victor. Without her, this wouldn't have been possible. Nor without Nix, whose power had saved my life here and who had forced me to take Del's power. Without my *deirfiúr*, I'd had no chance.

I funneled more of Del's magic into Victor, letting Del's power of death flow through me and into him. I held on to the memory of her as we finished Victor.

Finally, he collapsed into a pile of stone. The sickly scent of rot that followed his magic dissipated on the air.

The night grew silent.

On shaky legs, I climbed to my feet and stumbled over to the massive pile of rock. It sat on a bed of gray stone dust. I felt no magic in it, nor any life.

*Victor was dead.*

I left the Black Fort immediately, returning to Glencarrough just in time to see the black fog of Victor's circle of power disappear. Bodies were strewn everywhere, and demons fled on foot. They must have felt their master's death. The Shifters wouldn't let them get far.

I had won, but I felt no sense of victory. The tears that had dried threatened to return, but I swallowed them back hard. I needed to find my friends. To find out… if anyone else had died.

I stepped around the great crevice. Golden light flowed from it, no longer turning black from Victor's polluting touch. The melted Gundestrop cauldron still repressed my magic and everyone else's. They'd have to tear that out. Dermot's body lay nearby, torn to pieces.

The fire dragonet fluttered to hover in front of me. His brethren joined him—water, stone, and smoke—all flitting around me.

"Thanks, guys," I said. "Or girls."

They flew close enough to brush my shoulders, then turned and headed away, off to wherever they lived.

"Cass!" Aidan's voice sounded through the din.

I turned to follow the voice. He ran toward me, blood streaming down his face and arms, his chest soaked with it. But at least he was walking.

A body slammed into mine from the side, wrapping slender arms around me.

Nix.

"You're okay!" she cried. "You just left. You didn't take me with you!"

"I wasn't strong enough to take more than Victor." I had also been so angry and distraught that I hadn't stopped to think. I hugged her back. Hard. "He's dead."

She pulled back, tears streaming down her face and her eyes bright. But she looked almost…happy. "Del's body disappeared."

Shock, then hope, flared in me. "What? How?"

"She turned blue, then poof, she was gone."

"Holy shit. Only demons are supposed to disappear."

"And Del."

My mind raced. "This is good, right? It means she's not truly dead."

Nix nodded frantically. "I think so. I *have* to think so."

Aidan stepped up behind me and wrapped an arm around my waist, leaning down to envelop me. I could feel his relief that I was okay. It flowed through me as well. I had Nix and Aidan.

I glanced around, catching sight of Connor and Claire. They, too, were covered in blood. Connor was sitting on the ground, a shirt pressed to his head. Emile was sitting on the steps, Ralph and Rufus on his shoulders. One of his arms hung at an odd angle, but at least he was upright.

In the far corner, I saw Corin and Alton, from the League of FireSouls. They looked beat to hell, but alive.

"What are the casualties?" I asked.

"Not sure," Aidan said. "Several Shifters dead. They aren't used to fighting in human form. Elenora is fine, relatively speaking. She's vicious in any form."

Mordaca and Aerdeca approached. Aerdeca's white combat apparel was entirely soaked red with blood. I couldn't make out any rips in the fabric. Her gaze was hard, her mind still clearly steeped in battle.

So the blood wasn't hers. Demon blood. Go Aerdeca.

Mordaca was spotlessly clean, but her quiver was empty. I had no doubt that she had taken out a demon with every shot.

"You do know how to throw a party." Mordaca's voice was deadpan.

A weak grin tried and failed to pull at my mouth. Until Del was back—*if* Del came back—I didn't think I'd be able to smile.

"Thank you for coming," I said.

"We knew what was at stake," Aerdeca said. "Did you kill him?"

I nodded sharply, thinking of the pile of stone back at the Black Fort. I'd be going back there and dumping it all into the sea. "He is dead."

"Good." They nodded and departed. Not much for conversation, those two. But I was grateful for their help.

Corin approached, her short blonde hair flecked with blood. The sword that hung loosely at her side was coated as well, though it was hard to tell if there was any on her red armor.

"Is it over?" she asked.

"Yes," I said. "How are your people?"

"Our numbers are accounted for," she said. "There are some ghastly wounds, but we've trained long and hard with weapons. We'll all survive."

I nodded, relieved but unsurprised. FireSouls often became handy with weapons since we didn't want to use our magic and possibly reveal our signatures.

"Thank you for the help," I said.

She nodded, then departed. I was thankful. I couldn't bear to make small talk right now. Not with the question of Del still looming. My chest felt empty. Nix looked like she was about to fall over.

I turned to Aidan, about to request that we leave, when Elenora approached. Her dress was torn, and she was spotted with blood.

Irritation and the beginning of anger seethed in my chest. I wanted to blame her for Del's death. If she'd believed me when I'd first come to her, maybe all this wouldn't have happened.

*It is fated.*

Aethelred's words echoed in my mind. I shoved the voice, and my irritation, aside.

"Is Amara all right?" I asked before Elenora could speak.

"Yes. She's in the castle with the other children. The demons didn't reach them."

Relief made my shoulder muscles relax just slightly. Thank magic. Something to be happy about.

Elenora handed me a leather bag that I hadn't noticed her carrying.

"These are yours," she said.

I took the bag and peered inside. The twin obsidian daggers they'd taken from me. I didn't bother thanking her, just met her gaze.

"You've destroyed him?" Elenora asked.

"Yes. You believe me now?"

She nodded sharply. "I do. We should have taken the threat more seriously, but his parents were killed so long ago." She turned and gestured to the crack in the ground. "And the Stone of Power. It's been millennia since anyone has seen it. It'd become a myth to us. Not truly real, anyway."

"The Alpha Council was complacent in their power," Aidan said. "You spent too much time on the trappings of government and the appearance of strength."

I thought of their grand entryway and Council room, the priceless works of art. The round table and bureaucracy. Aidan was right. They'd lost sight of what really mattered.

Elenora inclined her head. "You are right, Origin. We must reassess." Her gaze met mine. "But in the meantime, you are pardoned. The Alpha Council will not interfere in your life or report you to the Order of the Magica for being a FireSoul. They will all be sworn to silence about what you are."

"They'd better be," I snapped. I didn't have the patience to be grateful. Once upon a time, a pardon from the Alpha Council would have meant the world to me.

Now, it was my due. They owed me this after what I'd sacrificed. After what Del had sacrificed.

Elenora didn't look at Nix, and if she knew Nix was a FireSoul, she didn't say. Nix was safe, though. None of the FireSouls who'd been here today faced any threat from the Alpha Council.

We were safe. Whatever that meant.

# CHAPTER SIXTEEN

The next evening, Nix and I sat on the floor of my trove, drinking PBR and staring blindly at my treasures. There was so much hope and fear in the room that it was hard to fit words in, too.

After the fight, we'd flown back to Magic's Bend on Aidan's jet and immediately gone to see Aethelred, who'd done his seer thing for us. For free, since he'd felt so badly about Del.

"So you believe him?" Nix asked.

"Yeah." I took a sip of the beer, thinking about Aethelred's prophecy that Del would return. "He was right the first time. And seers are always right."

We knew that fact; it was just hard to believe because we'd seen her take her last breath. And we wanted it to be true so badly. We *needed* her to be all right.

"I have to believe him," Nix said. "Otherwise, I don't think I can keep going. It's like there's a giant rock lodged in my chest."

"She'll be back," I said. And I believed it, too. This was all fated. And Del didn't feel dead. I'd know it if she were truly gone.

She wasn't.

"So that means we succeeded," Nix said.

"I think so."

Victor was gone. The Chalice of Youth was safe in the Museum of Magical History. The Shifters had the HeartStone back and were repairing the damage to the cavern that protected the Stone of Power. Whatever evil he'd tried to set loose on the world was stopped.

Knowing that Victor was dead felt like a million pounds had been lifted off my shoulders. There was no more Monster stalking us.

I leaned against Nix, letting her warmth flow into me and relax the rest of my muscles.

We were safe. For the first time in our lives, we were safe.

It didn't take long for Nix and me to get sick of sitting on my trove floor. Without Del, it just wasn't the same. So we'd polished off our beers and headed down to Potions & Pastilles.

On the plane ride home, I'd healed everyone's wounds by mirroring Aidan's healing gift. Connor wasn't opening up the bar to the public for the night, but he'd said we could come by. Aidan was at his place, getting cleaned up, so I'd texted him to let him know where we were.

The sun was setting as Nix and I walked down the street to P & P, sending a warm orange glow over the city street and the park to our right. As usual, there was no traffic in this part of town, so it was just me and Nix. It was weird to be walking without Del, but she'd be back. I kept repeating it to myself. It was true. I just had to believe it.

When we reached P & P, the glow from the hanging lights shined out the windows and welcomed us. There was a *Closed* sign on the door, which I ignored as I pushed it open and headed inside, and was enveloped by the scent of coffee and whisky. It went together well.

Connor grinned from behind the bar where he was mixing something in a glass.

"I'm experimenting here," he said.

"Excellent," I said. "Can't wait to try it."

We joined him at the bar, taking stools right in front of his mixing station. Whatever was in the glass looked like warm amber fire.

He popped a cherry in it and pushed it toward me. "Give it a try."

I nodded and took a sip, wincing slightly at the burn. It was no PBR, that was for sure, but the aftertaste was good. The second sip went down easier.

"I like it," I said as Claire pushed through the kitchen door into the bar area.

She held a platter with a big chocolate cake and grinned when she saw us. "Just in time! We have cake."

"Cake and whiskey?" Nix asked. "Sounds good to me."

We ate and drank, always conscious of Del's missing presence, but I was determined to cherish what I had. When Aidan entered the bar, I could feel him before he even spoke. I spun around on my barstool to see him walking through the door.

I hopped off the stool and met him near the door, then pushed him out into the street. The sun had just set, but the night glowed with a soft warmth that felt like a hug.

As the door swung shut behind us, I leaned up to kiss him. He bent down to meet me, pressing his warm lips to mine. I savored the touch, then pulled away.

"You look better," I said. Now that he'd washed the blood out of his hair and put on fresh clothes, it looked like he hadn't been in a fight to the death at all.

"So do you," he said. "Aethelred had good news?"

"Yeah." I glanced through the window at my friends, and gratitude hit me for all that I had. Sadness and fear for Del lurked just below the surface, but I refused to embrace it.

I met Aidan's gaze, my heart swelling with how much he meant to me. "Remember how you said you loved me?"

"I do." His gaze was serious.

"I love you, too."

A grin broke out over his face, and he leaned down and pressed his lips to mine. I threw my arms around his neck and kissed him back, pouring everything I had into it.

When he pulled away, I grinned too. Why had I been so confused about this? It was so obvious.

"You're not going to regret it," he said.

"You're right." I could just barely hear my friends through the glass as they chatted and ate chocolate cake. I had them all. Del would find her way back. I'd do everything I could to help. And we were free. For the first time in our lives, we were free.

I swung an arm around Aidan's waist and said, "Come on. They've got cake and whiskey, and we deserve to celebrate."

# THANK YOU FOR READING!

Want to find out how Cass and her *deirfiúr* got the money to start their shop? Sign up for my newsletter at www.LinseyHall.com/subscribe to get a free, exclusive copy of *Hidden Magic,* which is only available to subscribers.

Reviews are *so* helpful to authors. I really appreciate all reviews, both positive and negative.

# AUTHOR'S NOTE

Thank you for reading *Infinite Magic*. I hope you enjoyed reading it as much as I enjoyed writing it. The Dragon's Gift series combines my two lives—I am both a writer and an archaeologist.

As with my other stories, *Infinite Magic* features historical sites and mythological influences. Some of them you've seen in my other books and some are new.

One of the new historical sites was that of Vlad the Impaler's castle in Romania. When I needed to think of a new headquarters for Victor Orriodor, it seemed like the ideal place for him. Vlad III was the Prince of Wallachia in the 15th century in what is now Romania. He had a nasty habit of impaling his enemies on spikes, hence his name. I haven't had the good fortune to visit the castle, however, so I took many liberties with its construction.

The other major historical and mythological influences in the book can be seen in the scene where Cass goes searching for the broch. She receives help along the way from some characters from Scottish mythology. Caesg's are Highland mermaids who are part woman, part salmon. The Nuckelavee is a terrifying monster from the Orkney Islands, in northern Scotland. I moved him south for the purpose of the story because he was just too good not to include. The Bauchan is a type of Scottish hobgoblin, who is known to be helpful when necessary. There are images and links to more information about these creatures on my Pinterest page (just search Linsey Hall on Pinterest-it'll be easy to find).

By far, brochs are one of my favorite types of archaeological sites. These iron age round towers can be found all over northern and western Scotland. They aren't generally found in the central part of the Scottish Highlands, where Glencarrough is located, but I put one there just so that I could write about it. There is no common consensus amongst archaeologists about why brochs were built and how they were used. Cass thinks to herself that the broch at Glencarrough would have been an excellent defensive structure because that is a natural assessment of a big stone tower. However, there isn't much archaeological evidence to support that brochs were universally used for this purpose, and many archaeologists today doubt that they were used for defense. You can check out my Pinterest page for more images and links if you are interested.

Ralph and Rufus, the two rats who befriended Emile, are not mythological creatures, but they deserve a place in the Author's Note. Ralph and Rufus were two very clever rats that I lived with while I was in college. They belonged to my friend Emily, who is a real animal whisperer. I did not consciously name Emile for Emily.

He first appeared in *Mirror Mage* as a captured FireSoul, and he was male. When it came time for him to reappear in *Eternal Magic*, I decided to give him the ability to talk to animals. Hence, Ralph and Rufus appeared. But when it came time to name him, I chose the first name that popped into my mind—Emile. It was several weeks later that I realized I probably named Emile for Emily. I was writing quickly because the story was flowing and I just went with it. In hindsight, Emile is clearly Emily.

That's it for the historical and archaeological influences in *Infinite Magic*. But one of the most important things about the *Dragon's Gift* series is Cass's relationship with the artifacts and the sense of responsibility she feels to protect them. I spoke about this in the Author's Note for the other books in the series, so this part might be repetitive for some folks (feel free to quit now if so), but I want to include it in each of my Author's Notes because it's so important to me.

I knew I had a careful line to tread when writing these books—combining the ethics of archaeology with the fantasy aspect of treasure hunting isn't always easy.

There is a big difference between these two activities. As much as I value artifacts, they are not treasure. Not even the gold artifacts. They are pieces of our history that contain valuable information, and as such, they belong to all of us. Every artifact that is excavated should be properly conserved and stored in a museum so that everyone can have access to our history. No single person can own history, and I believe very strongly that individuals should not own artifacts.

Treasure hunting is the pursuit of artifacts for personal gain.

So why did I make Cass Cleraux a treasure hunter? I'd have loved to call her an archaeologist, but nothing about Cass's work is like archaeology. Archaeology is a very laborious, painstaking process—and it certainly doesn't involve selling artifacts. That wouldn't work for the fast-paced, adventurous series that I had planned for *Dragon's Gift*. Not to mention the fact that dragons are famous for coveting treasure. Considering where Cass got her skills, it just made sense to call her a treasure hunter (though I really like to think of her as a magic hunter). Even though I write urban fantasy, I strive for accuracy. Cass doesn't engage in archaeological practices—therefore, I cannot call her an archaeologist. I also have a duty as an archaeologist to properly represent my field and our goals—namely, to protect and share history. Treasure hunting doesn't do this. One of the biggest battles that archaeology faces today is protecting cultural heritage from thieves.

I debated long and hard about not only what to call Cass, but also about how she would do her job. I wanted it to involve all the cool things we think about when we think about archaeology—namely, the Indiana Jones stuff, whether it's real or not. Because that stuff is fun, and my main goal is to write a fun book. But I didn't know quite how to do that while still staying within the bounds of my own ethics. I can cut myself and other writers some slack because this is fiction, but I couldn't go too far into smash-and-grab treasure hunting.

I consulted some of my archaeology colleagues to get their take, which was immensely helpful. Wayne Lusardi, the State Maritime Archaeologist for Michigan, and Douglas Inglis and Veronica Morris, both archaeologists for Interactive Heritage, were immensely helpful with ideas. My biggest problem was figuring out how to have Cass steal artifacts from tombs and then sell them and still sleep at night. Everything I've just said is pretty counter to this, right?

That's where the magic comes in. Cass isn't after the artifacts themselves (she puts them back where she found them, if you recall)—she's after the magic that the artifacts contain. She's more of a magic hunter than a treasure hunter. That solved a big part of my problem. At least she was putting the artifacts back. Though that's not proper archaeology (especially the damage she sometimes causes, which she always goes back to fix), I could let it pass. At least it's clear that she believes she shouldn't keep the artifact or harm the site. But the SuperNerd in me said, "Well, that magic is part of the artifact's context. It's important to the artifact and shouldn't be removed and sold."

Now *that* was a problem. I couldn't escape my SuperNerd self, so I was in a real conundrum. Fortunately, that's where the immensely intelligent Wayne Lusardi came in. He suggested that the magic could have an expiration date. If the magic wasn't used before it decayed, it could cause huge problems. Think explosions and tornado spells run amok. It could ruin the entire site, not to mention possibly cause injury and death. That would be very bad.

So now you see why Cass Clereaux didn't just steal artifacts to sell them. Not only is selling the magic cooler, it's also better from an ethical standpoint, especially if the magic was going to cause problems in the long run. These aren't perfect solutions—the perfect solution would be sending in a team of archaeologists to carefully record the site and remove the dangerous magic—but that wouldn't be a very fun book. Hopefully this was a good compromise that you enjoyed (and that my old professors don't hang their heads over).

Thank you so much for reading *Infinite Magic*, and if you've made it this far in the Author's Note, thank you for reading this as well! It's an important part of the story and I appreciate when folks take the time to learn about the archaeological influences in my books. I hope you'll stay with Cass, Nix, and Del on their journey, because it's not done yet!

# GLOSSARY

Alpha Council - There are two governments that enforce law for supernaturals—the Alpha Council and the Order of the Magica. The Alpha Council governs all shifters. They work cooperatively with Alpha Council when necessary - for example, when capturing FireSouls.

Bauchan - A type of Scottish hobgoblin who can be tricksy or helpful depending upon the circumstance.

Blood Sorceress - A type of Magica who can create magic using blood.

Ceasg - A Highland mermaid. Half woman, half salmon.

Conjurer - A Magica who uses magic to create something from nothing. They cannot create magic, but if there is magic around them, they can put that magic into their conjuration.

Dark Magic - The kind that is meant to harm. It's not necessarily bad, but it often is.

*Deirfiúr* - Sisters in Irish.

Demons - Often employed to do evil. They live in various hells but can be released upon the earth if you know how to get to them and then get them out. If they are killed on earth, they are sent back to their hell.

Dragon Sense - A FireSoul's ability to find treasure. It is an internal sense pulls them toward what they seek. It is easiest to find gold, but they can find anything or anyone that is valued by someone.

Elemental Mage – A rare type of mage who can manipulate all of the elements.

Enchanted Artifacts – Artifacts can be imbued with magic that lasts after the death of the person who put the magic into the artifact (unlike a spell that has not been put into an artifact—these spells disappear after the Magica's death). But magic is not stable. After a period of time—hundreds or thousands of years depending on the circumstance—the magic will degrade. Eventually, it can go bad and cause many problems.

Fire Mage – A mage who can control fire.

FireSoul - A very rare type of Magica who shares a piece of the dragon's soul. They can locate treasure and steal the gifts (powers) of other supernaturals. With practice, they can manipulate the gifts they steal, becoming the strongest of that gift. They are despised and feared. If they are caught, they are thrown in the Prison of Magical Miscreants.

Hearth Witch – A Magica who is versed in magic relating to hearth and home. They are often good and potions and protective spells and are also very perceptive when on their own turf.

Magica - Any supernatural who has the power to create magic—witches, sorcerers, mages. All are governed by the Order of the Magica.

Mirror Mage - A Magica who can temporarily borrow the powers of other supernaturals. They can mimick the powers as long as the are near the other supernatural. Or they can hold onto the power, but once they are away from the other supernatural, they can only use it once.

Nuckelavee - A horrifying monster. He is part horse, part man. Though he is a monster from the sea, he rides on land for part of the year.

The Origin - The descendent of the original alpha shifter. They are the most powerful shifter and can turn into any species.

Order of the Magica - There are two governments that enforce law for supernaturals—the Alpha Council and the Order of the Magica. The Order of the Magica govern all Magica. They work cooperatively with Alpha Council when necessary - for example, when capturing FireSouls.

Phantom - A type of supernatural that is similar to a ghost. They are incorporeal. They feed off the misery and pain of others, forcing them to relive their greatest nightmares and fears. They do not have a fully functioning mind like a human or supernatural. Rather, they are a shadow of their former selves. Half bloods are extraordinarily rare.

Seeker - A type of supernatural who can find things. FireSouls often pass off their dragon sense as being Seeker power.

Shifter - A supernatural who can turn into an animal. All are governed by the Alpha Council.

Transporter - A type of supernatural who can travel anywhere. Their power is limited and must regenerate after each use.

# ABOUT LINSEY

Before becoming a writer, Linsey Hall was a nautical archaeologist who studied shipwrecks from Hawaii and the Yukon to the UK and the Mediterranean. She credits fantasy and historical romances with her love of history and her career as an archaeologist. After a decade of tromping around the globe in search of old bits of stuff that people left lying about, she settled down and started penning her own adventure novels. Her Dragon's Gift series draws upon her love of history and the paranormal elements that she can't help but include.

Copyright 2016 by Linsey Hall
Published by Bonnie Doon Press LLC

Linsey@LinseyHall.com
www.LinseyHall.com
https://twitter.com/HiLinseyHall
https://www.facebook.com/LinseyHallAuthor

BONNIE
DOON
PRESS

ISBN 978-1-942085-53-9